Caris was going crazy. She needed a cigarette. She needed...

Alex.

She could hear his footsteps, as familiar to her as her own heartbeat, coming down the hall. She held her breath.

There was a soft knock and she was out of bed, opening the door, before she'd even decided whether to let him in.

He stood there, his gaze warm, his smile wicked. "Somehow I knew you'd be awake. And tense." His smile deepened. "I have just the thing to help."

"Oh?" Her heart leapt, and warmth settled in her belly. When he handed her a small box wrapped in red tissue paper, she was hardly able to mask her disappointment. "What's this?"

"I suspect it's not what either of us *really* needs, but..." His shrug spoke of regret. "I hope it helps with your craving for nicotine." He picked up her hand and brushed his lips across her knuckles before turning to walk back down the hall.

She could only stare after him, wishing she'd had the nerve to pull him into her room and lock the door behind them, and revel in what they *both* craved. Shakily, she ripped into the box.

Packages of gum—everything from sugar-free spearmint to double-bubble—spilled out. Caris was still smiling when she went back to bed and resigned herself to a sleepless night.

Lisa E. Arlt has been writing since she could hold a crayon, but life and a career in the U.S. foreign service waylaid her a while. Then one bleak winter day in Prague, Czech Republic, she began writing her first romance novel, and the rest is history.

Although she still enjoys the career that takes her to many fascinating places, writing romance is her true life's work. Lisa has recently been posted to Brussels, Belgium, where she now lives with her husband and two dogs.

SMOKE AND MIRRORS
Lisa E. Arlt

Harlequin Books

TORONTO • NEW YORK • LONDON
AMSTERDAM • PARIS • SYDNEY • HAMBURG
STOCKHOLM • ATHENS • TOKYO • MILAN
MADRID • WARSAW • BUDAPEST • AUCKLAND

For my husband—
who taught me "happily ever after" isn't just in books.
Thanks to the Washington Romance Writers
for making me feel at home.
And special thanks to my critique partners Laurin Wittig,
Diane Gaston, Catherine Abbott-Anderson,
Jo Anne Gild, Karin L. Schroeder and Yvonne Pinney
for keeping me honest.

ISBN 0-373-25780-5

SMOKE AND MIRRORS

Copyright © 1998 by Lisa E. Arlt.

Printed in U.S.A.

1

CARIS JOHNSON DECIDED that today might not be the best day for her to quit smoking. She had heard people say they would kill for a cigarette, but she had never really believed it.

Until now.

She gripped the airplane armrest, balancing on a razor sharp edge of fear. The plane dropped suddenly, sucking the air from her lungs. She moaned, feeling a potent mixture of panic and airsickness. Her eyes slitted against the nausea, she shot a glance at her traveling companion.

Harrison J. Peters III, Esquire, slept peacefully, a slight smile on his pinched and aging face, completely oblivious to the turbulence and Caris's panic.

Good. It was never wise to show weakness, especially not to the man capable of deciding her entire professional future.

The small plane rattled and shook ominously. Caris stiffened, stretching her toes straight ahead as though she were trying to touch the ground.

She vowed that as soon as she made partner at Harrison, Harrison, Joffrey and Peters, Attorneys-at-Law, one of the most prestigious law firms in Washington, D.C., she would never get on another airplane as long as she lived.

It was hard to believe she had lobbied for this trip.

When she'd first learned that her firm's newly developed Real Estate Division would be bidding on a partnership with Navarro Investments for the creation of a new beachfront resort community on Navarro Island, Caris had been sure this was her ticket to the first female partnership in the exclusive male firm. She was on the phone immediately, calling in every favor owed her. Bookkeeping "mistakenly" sent a copy of her sizable billable hours to each of the partners. Dozens of clients chose that day to bombard the switchboard with calls expressing their satisfaction with attorney Caris Johnson's hard work and dedication.

But the clincher was the fax Mr. Joffrey received on his private line from Yale University. It was a copy of Caris's senior thesis and it was on the acquisition and establishment of beach-resort communities.

Of course, in the eight years since she'd graduated, Caris hadn't even visited a beach, let alone considered the complications of building a new resort. But she wasn't about to let a little thing like inexperience stop her. She had always been an expert at flinging herself into a new situation and landing on two-inch heels with barely a wobble.

Her father used to call her Kitten and Caris knew it wasn't because she was soft and cuddly. She had never been soft and cuddly, not even as a child. In her family, she was definitely the odd person out.

But at Harrison, Harrison, Joffrey and Peters, a place where "snake in the grass" was considered a complimentary term, Caris felt right at home.

The tiny commuter plane shook again, and Harrison rubbed the bald ring on the top of his head with a wrinkled hand, making a sound somewhere between a snore and a grumble. She shot him an irritated look.

Her enthusiasm for the trip had dimmed considerably when she discovered Harrison J. Peters would be the other member of the team. Harrison J. Peters hated smokers, and Caris was a smoker.

Not just a smoker but a heavy smoker. Her roommate had often joked that if it weren't for the Marlboro man and Juan the coffee guy, Caris never would have made it through Yale Law School.

No one at the firm knew she was a smoker. No one of importance, anyway. She'd spent the past few years at the law firm smoking in the ladies' room, then covering up the smell with a unique mix of Lysol and Chanel No 5.

The secretaries all knew she smoked, of course. It was impossible to hide the telltale blue smoke rising from the stall, but they kept her secret, either to remain her friend or to avoid becoming her enemy.

But Caris knew it would be impossible to hide her habit during a two-week trip to a remote island off the coast of Texas, especially from Harrison. All it would take would be one breath drawn through Harrison's keen, aristocratic nostrils and her secret would be out.

She had thought it was an easy decision for her to make; cigarettes or her professional future. But now, sitting on the plane six hours after her last cigarette, her composure and sanity slowly crumbling, Caris didn't think she was going to make it.

She felt like screaming. Her head pounded and her jaw ached from chewing gum. The scent of Juicy Fruit was starting to make her sick. If only she hadn't been so sure she'd have no difficulty quitting and had bought some of those nicotine patches.

She glanced surreptitiously at Harrison J. Peters III. He was still asleep.

If she hurried, she might be able to slip back to the bathroom and make her own cigarette using toilet tissue and the tobacco grounds she scrounged up from the bottom of her purse.

Harrison shifted slightly, mumbling in his sleep. She leaned closer, curious about the subconscious murmurings of a senior partner.

He mumbled again and she smiled. She could have sworn she heard him say, "Hostile takeover." The man couldn't be all bad if he dreamed contracts and sales in his sleep.

Her ears popped and her stomach dropped. The pilot was beginning his descent.

"Please fasten your seat belts," the flight attendant said. Nearly all of the fourteen passengers complied.

Harrison stirred in the seat next to her, stretching his bony frame, barely missing her breasts with his elbow.

She smiled, trying to camouflage the demons of her nicotine withdrawal.

"Are we there yet?" Harrison drawled, his southern accent oozing out strong and unfiltered.

"Not yet." She looked out the window, wondering if they had smoke detectors in the bathrooms in the airport. Or if they even had bathrooms. If it wasn't for the offshore oil rigs that had been built in the seventies, then capped and abandoned in the eighties, Navarro Island probably wouldn't even have an airport.

"Nothing but water down there." Harrison strained to see over her shoulder and she slumped unobtrusively, knowing the man hated to be reminded of his short stature.

Caris was only five-eight, not too tall considering this day of six-foot female models. But three-fourths of the partnership of HHJ and P—Mr. Joffrey excluded—were the same height as Caris. Caris guessed it was the result of generations of intermarrying among the law firm's partners. If Caris were to wear high heels she would dwarf them.

Caris never wore high heels.

Not even on days when she felt ultrafeminine, wishing to add a slight sway to her generous hips. To Caris, feeling sexy wasn't worth the risk of annoying a senior partner.

"We must be getting close, though," Harrison said, scratching his gray-stubbled chin. "I think I see land."

"As I said, it's less than a one-hour flight from Galveston," Caris said. "Once the resort is established, we'll be able to charter flights from Houston, forgoing the inconvenience of these tiny commuter planes." *And the terror.*

Harrison smiled indulgently. "That's my Caris. Always does her research."

She smiled, feeling the coral lipstick on her lips crack. Caris wasn't anyone's Caris.

"You brought the background data on Alex Navarro?" Harrison asked.

"In my briefcase."

"Good. We'll need it." Harrison shook his balding head. "I still don't understand why Navarro is in such a hurry. Whoever heard of negotiating a land deal without even seeing the land? I hope you're up to the challenge."

"You can count on me, Harrison."

Harrison snorted disbelievingly, but Caris barely heard him. Excitement licked through her veins at the legal battle ahead of her. Her adrenaline rose to meet the challenge. Mentally, she ticked through the information she'd already memorized.

Alexander Navarro. Recently resigned from a high-powered position as a financial analyst for a powerful Wall Street brokerage company to return to Navarro Island. Caris doubted it was grief over his father's recent death that prompted Alex's abrupt change of lifestyle; rumor had it that the two Navarros hadn't exchanged a pleasant word in more than a decade. More likely it was the presidency of Navarro Investments that drew Alex.

Although Alex's brother, Michael, and sister, Kate, owned equal shares in the family business, it was Alex who held all of the power. Caris doubted she'd even get to meet the other Navarros. Michael was in the final year of his Master's of Business at Harvard, and Kate was the wife of one of the richest men in Houston. And neither of them appeared to be grieving the death of their father, either.

It was Alex Navarro who would decide which investors got a stake in the resort. And whether Caris would get her partnership.

Although she was glad for the opportunity, Caris couldn't help wondering why Navarro Investments was even looking for a partner. Virgin beach properties in the United States weren't discovered every day. Especially not beaches with an underwater trove of sunken Spanish galleons ringing half of the island. Three companies in Galveston already ran profitable dive trips to Navarro Island, but the ferryboat ride from Galveston to Navarro could make even the hardiest sailors lose their breakfast.

If Navarro built his own resort on the island and took away the need for the two-hour ferry ride, he'd have a built-in clientele who'd pay highly for the privilege of diving in nearly untouched waters and staying on the secluded island. All of this for barely an hour's flight from Houston. So what did he need a partner for?

Navarro's invitation hinted at a company about to go under, but Navarro Investments had spent nearly a decade on the Fortune 500 list. They'd made a killing during the oil boom of the seventies. And Alex Navarro had left a six-figure salary to come here. If the Navarros had fallen from grace, Caris would know about it.

Her mind returned to the man behind the business. Alex Navarro. Alex was one of the most cunning graduates of Harvard University. But Caris held that distinguished title coming out of Yale. They were evenly matched.

She grinned. The man didn't stand a chance. Not when her whole future could rest on this one deal. She would chew him up and eat him for breakfast.

And then afterward, she'd smoke him like a cigarette.

Harrison stood, ignoring the seat-belt sign, the sharp slope of the plane floor and the flight attendant's dirty look. "I'm going to go make myself more official-looking. Can't meet our opponent looking unshaven now, can we?"

Caris smiled politely as he made his way aft, holding on to the seat tops for balance. She wondered if she looked as bad as she felt and that was Harrison's subtle way of telling her to powder her nose.

Caris shrugged, unwilling to waste any time thinking about her appearance.

Across the aisle, a woman giggled. Caris looked her way, then wished she hadn't. The woman, blond, giggly and jiggly, sat on a man's lap. Her hands were on his chest, his hands were inside her blouse.

Honeymooners, if the glittery rock on the woman's left hand and their lustful, satisfied grins were anything to go by. The woman giggled again.

Didn't they have any shame?

Caris glanced out her window, then back to the couple again. If she were in love, she'd never parade herself in public like that.

Her stomach clenched and her chest tightened.

If she were in love…

At the rate she was going, she'd never be in love. Caris never even had time to date. Her life had been spent working and studying and trying to get ahead.

But wasn't that what she wanted? Of course it was, so why was she doubting herself?

Must be the cigarettes.

To distract herself, Caris reached into her suit pocket and pulled out the phone messages she hadn't had a chance to answer before her flight. Most were things her secretary, Linda, could take care of, except for one. Matthew Clark.

She grinned, remembering her socially conscious law-school friend. It had been a year since his last phone call and Caris knew what that meant. Yet another of Matthew's law clerks had abandoned social justice for a higher-paying position and he was hoping she'd be able to find him a replacement.

When would Matthew ever learn? Money was what drove the world, not social conscience.

She'd call him when she got back. She could probably find him a starry-eyed law clerk willing to trade some legal assistance for experience to put on a résumé. At least until student loans came due and the person jumped ship.

The plane dropped sharply and Caris gasped. The woman

across the aisle giggled nervously and wrapped her arms around her husband's neck.

Caris squeezed her eyes shut wishing she had someone to hold on to.

The plane dipped again and she decided that, yes, at this moment, she would gladly kill for a cigarette.

ALEXANDER NAVARRO watched the commuter plane glide over the gulf and settle gently on the single runway at Navarro Airport. The tropical breeze blew the sound of the engine away, making the plane as quiet as a glider.

Alex tapped one finger nervously on the silver Land Cruiser he'd borrowed for today's meeting. "That's them."

Michael didn't answer and Alex turned to see his younger brother sitting in the passenger seat, staring morosely at his Rolex watch.

Although Alex and Michael had the same dark hair and tall, muscular build, Alex had often heard Michael referred to as a pale imitation of his older brother. Alex wondered if Michael had heard that also, and if that was perhaps the reason they hadn't gotten along over the last ten years.

"Did you hear me?" Alex asked, sharper than he'd intended.

"I heard you." Michael stepped out of the four-by-four, flicking a disparaging finger at it. "What's going on here, Alex?"

Alex's stomach tightened. "What do you mean?"

"What happened to the limo?"

He forced himself not to react. "I told you, it's in the shop."

"Uh-huh." Michael took a step toward him. "And the chauffeur's on vacation?"

Alex consciously controlled his breathing, knowing his brother was watching for any sign of discomfort. "Yes."

Michael cocked his head. "Why don't you tell me the truth, Alex."

"I am telling you the truth."

"Of course you are." Michael didn't sound convinced.

Alex didn't blame him. As far as cover stories went, his had holes big enough to fly a commuter plane through. But he hadn't had time to think of anything better when Michael showed up at the house unexpectedly last night, throwing all of Alex's carefully plotted plans into disarray. How could Alex have explained missing servants and a house emptied of everything valuable without telling Michael the truth— that Navarro Investments was broke. Once their father's will was out of probate the whole world would know that fact and his bargaining power with Harrison, Harrison, Joffrey and Peters would disappear. Alex was in no hurry for that to happen.

He wished he could trust his brother with the truth, but Michael was too much of an opportunist for Alex to even consider it.

"Why is John pretending to be your butler?" Michael asked.

Alex took a deep breath. "Like I told you last night, Michael, John isn't pretending. I hired him."

"Yeah. Right."

Alex felt a drop of sweat slide down his spine toward the small of his back. If only Michael hadn't shown up last night. Alex shot a glance at his brother. Why had he come last night? He should be in the middle of finals. "Why are you here, Michael?"

Michael's hollow laugh barely disguised the nervous edge beneath it. "You make it sound like I'm not welcome in my own home."

"You haven't been home in years."

Michael glared at him. "Neither have you."

"Do you need money?"

"Is that the only way you think of me?" Michael flushed, beads of sweat coating his unlined forehead. "As some moneygrubbing pariah who only comes looking for a handout?"

Alex shrugged. This wasn't the time or place to go into what he thought of his younger brother.

"Maybe I just wanted to help out," Michael said.

Alex wished he could believe that. Past experience warned him to tread cautiously. "Forgive me for being skeptical, Michael, but—"

"I can help, Alex. I do have some experience in business matters. After all, I've almost got my MBA."

"Not if you keep leaving school like this."

Michael's cheeks reddened again and Alex almost expected him to stomp his feet like a petulant child. Instead, Michael took a deep breath and changed the subject. "Listen to me, Alex. We could make a killing. Nakashimi is willing to pay millions for the beach. We should just sell it outright and get the hell off this island."

Alex tasted the familiar bitterness he usually felt when he dealt with his brother. "Is that all you ever think about, Michael? Money?"

"Money makes the world go round," Michael said. "And you should know that better than most."

For a time, Alex had believed in Michael's creed. But that was a month ago, before his world had changed. Before his father died, leaving behind a business empire, a needy and quarreling family and a pocketful of secrets.

Alex leaned against the car still staring at the plane. Actually, he'd been dissatisfied with his life for the last two years. He'd been filled with an aching need, a nameless desire for something he couldn't envision. His father's death had clarified his thoughts and offered him the chance to start over again. A chance he gladly took, shucking his high-profile and high-powered career with barely a second thought.

But, so far, his life was still the same. Empty, meaningless and devoid of something he couldn't even describe. Alex wanted more.

More of what, he didn't know. He hadn't found it at Harvard, hadn't found it on Wall Street and he hadn't found it on Navarro Island, his birthplace. He was starting to wonder if he ever would.

"How much of a chance do I have of changing your mind?" Michael asked, ever the gambler.

"Probably as much chance as I have of changing yours."

Michael tightened his lips. "Don't start, Alex. I'm not in the mood."

"Don't you ever think about your future, Michael? There's more to life than parties and women. And why don't you tell me what you're really doing here? I know damn well you haven't come to help."

Michael swore. "You may be in charge of the family business, Alex, but you're not in charge of me."

For that, Alex was grateful. "You're not going to be twenty-four forever, Michael. One day you'll have to grow up, take some responsibility, use that MBA you're working so hard to get."

Michael shrugged his comments away. "Not today, Alex. Today, I'm still twenty-four and you handle the family business so well I don't even need to exist. Besides, when I do give you my input, you don't take it."

Alex frowned. Over the past few years, Michael hadn't offered any input about anything but his profit-sharing statement. "What input?"

"The beach."

Of course. Except it wasn't the beach resort that interested Michael. It was the money. "That again. Michael, the lawyers are landing. If we can come to an agreement, I'll make a deal with them."

Michael sighed, sounding more petulant than angry. "I'm not against making a deal, Alex, I just think you're making the wrong one. I can't believe you're willing to form a partnership with people you don't even know, when the Nakashimi Corporation has offered a hundred times more to purchase the land outright."

"How do you know how much they offered?"

Michael, who hadn't even set foot inside the Navarro offices since he left high school, had the sense to look embarrassed. "I must have heard you mention it."

More likely, he had searched Alex's home office after his arrival last night until he found the information he wanted. "Nakashimi plans to raze the town and empty the island of most of the people who live here," Alex said. "I'm trying to build the resort to give these people a reason to stay on the island, not an ultimatum to leave it."

"But this is a win-win situation."

"It's not my kind of win-win situation, Michael."

"Why do you care so much?" Anger overcame the coolness Michael had been trying so hard to project. "You haven't lived here in over ten years. And if the situation were reversed, the islanders would sell you out for a bottle of suntan lotion."

Although Alex had spent a decade in New York, he'd never stopped being an islander. But Michael had never understood anything as subtle as affection or loyalty. "What's your point, Michael?"

"If it were my company, I'd sell everything, buy a huge house in Hollywood and live a life of luxury until I either dropped dead or my money ran out."

Alex knew Michael meant every word he said. That was exactly what Michael would do if he were handed control of Navarro Investments. Michael wouldn't worry about anything but enjoying himself.

"While I'm president of Navarro Investments, I'll make the decisions." Alex softened his voice, trying to reason with his sibling. "There's more to this deal than you know, Michael." Much more, but Alex wasn't ready to tell his brother yet. Not when he still didn't know why Michael had shown up so unexpectedly last night.

Alex watched the small plane taxi toward the hangar. Although he suspected he'd never change Michael's mind, it didn't stop him from trying. "It's not just about money, Michael. It's about a way of life. The island is dying. We're losing people by the ferryload, and it's not going to get any better without help. We need to give people a reason to stay. The whole point of this merger is to buy the islanders a future, not sell their homeland.''

Michael tightened his fingers into a fist, an unconscious action Alex was sure his brother hadn't wanted him to see. ''You know what, Alex? I think you get a big kick out of being boss and having everyone bow down to you. Well, not me. You're just a man, Alex. Remember that. And you can fall just as easily as any other man.''

Alex raised one eyebrow, a coldly calculated look he'd honed during his final year at Harvard. ''Is that a threat, brother?''

Michael laughed, his expression changing from cutthroat to lighthearted scamp. ''I'd never fight you over money, Alex. You know that. Now, if it were a woman, that's another story.''

Alex stared at the plane, unwilling to watch the greed still shining in his brother's face.

''Here they come.'' He was about to meet the men who would change the future of Navarro Island.

''OUCH!'' Caris jumped as Harrison's briefcase hit her squarely on the rear.

''Sorry,'' Harrison mumbled, still using his case to nudge her forward. ''The early bird gets the worm.''

Caris gritted her teeth and moved down the aisle toward the door as quickly as she could, which wasn't easy, considering the other passengers were all trying to squeeze along the tiny aisle at the same time.

She stopped, allowing a mother to ease her two toddlers into the aisle ahead of her. Harrison bumped into her again. She held her ground, refusing to let anyone, even a senior partner, trample young children.

The woman smiled gratefully at her and whispered a shy thank-you.

Caris smiled back with an unfamiliar sense that she had done the right thing.

"Ouch!"

Harrison was pushing forward again, and this time she moved, grumbling internally.

A wave of hot, moist air blew over her from the opened airplane door and she felt her panty hose melt onto her legs. She had dressed professionally for the ride, clothed in a business suit, white linen blouse and leather flats, but she felt as rumpled as if she had spent the night asleep on a stack of law books.

She stood in the doorway, her eyes tearing from the white sunlight and the overwhelming heat.

Harrison pushed past her and barreled down the rolling gangplank, his movements making the metal staircase bounce.

Caris raised her eyes to the azure sky and whispered a silent prayer for a successful trip.

And a cigarette.

ALEX NOTICED the woman the second she exited the plane. The hairs on the back of his neck stood up and he shivered in the tropical heat.

She wasn't what Alex would consider classically beautiful. In fact, he wondered if she'd purposely tried to make herself appear less attractive than she actually was. Her blond hair was plastered to her head, cruelly anchored in a tight bun, a few wisps curling free.

She was clothed in a straight gray business suit, the colors and the style designed to mute her feminine appeal. The skirt fell to mid-knee and she wore sensible shoes. Her blouse was buttoned almost to her chin, yet he suspected she wore lace underneath.

Her face was pale, evidence of the rough landing for

which Navarro Island was famous. Her eyes were closed, her face raised in mute appeal to the sky. He wondered if her eyes were blue. She looked tired and he felt her fatigue as though it were his own.

He wondered who she was. And he wondered even more why he cared.

Caris stood at the top of the airplane gangplank. Her stomach grumbled both from hunger and the rough landing and she felt uncomfortably warm in her jacket. When she'd bought the suit, the saleslady had assured her the material was suitable for summer weather.

But this wasn't summer weather. This was the tropics, and she wondered if it was possible for a person to actually melt. If so, she'd soon be puddling down the gangplank, an oozing mass of gray cotton held together by a single strand of classic pearls, her only feminine indulgence.

As Caris's eyes opened, she realized Harrison was already striding across the tarmac toward two tall men. She rushed down the steps.

She ran across the tarmac, not caring how she looked, only knowing that she had to be with the men or they would push her out of the loop. She felt her hair loosening, wispy tendrils curling in escape from the severe bun that contained them. Her cheeks flushed, a mixture of heat and embarrassment. She held one hand on her bun, which was bouncing its way down her neck, while the other gripped her black leather briefcase.

Breathing rapidly, she pulled to a halt beside Harrison. When she looked up, she met and clung to dark eyes that saw all her secrets. The air left her lungs. The rest of the world disappeared, too, and there was only him.

The wind had ruffled his dark hair and she longed to brush it back with her fingertips. Would it feel rough, she wondered, or smooth as a lover's touch?

Reality intruded as Harrison nudged her arm. "And this

breathless young woman is Caris Johnson, another lawyer at our firm."

The man smiled at her, his gaze still holding hers. He reached out to shake her hand.

Both of Caris's hands were full, one with her briefcase, the other holding on to her hair clip, now dangling helplessly at the back of her neck. She had to make a choice. She pulled her hand back from her hair and extended it toward him.

The wind picked up, ruffling her blond tresses, and her hair clip succumbed to gravity and clattered to the ground. Her long hair, now completely unencumbered, floated behind her like a banner rustling in the breeze.

The man's eyes darkened further. She felt an unfamiliar heat burn in her belly.

His fingers, cool and strong, enveloped her hand. An electric current whipped up her arm. She flushed further, her eyes widening in confusion and uneasiness.

The man seemed equally affected, his grip tightening slightly. "It's a pleasure to meet you, Ms. Johnson," he said, his voice a deep, pleasant rumble.

"Who are you?"

She blushed as she realized she had spoken aloud.

"I am Alex Navarro, at your service." He bowed slightly, still holding her hand.

She couldn't seem to catch her breath. Her face felt hot, her body even hotter. For the first time in her professional life, she had no idea what to say.

"And I'm Michael Navarro." Michael pushed their hands apart, capturing and holding hers like a trophy. He bent and kissed the back of her pale hand.

Startled by Michael Navarro's presence, Caris smiled, amused by his macho display. Michael Navarro was safe. She could handle him with no problem.

On the other hand, Alex scared her senseless. Or maybe it wasn't fear that skittered up her spine so disturbingly but a different, more primal emotion she had never before experienced.

He moved toward her and she stepped back, pulling her hand from Michael's.

Alex bent over and picked up her hair clip. He handed it to her with a smile. "I believe this is yours."

"Thank you."

He turned toward Harrison. "If you'll give me your luggage receipts, we'll have someone retrieve your suitcases."

Harrison dug into his breast pocket. Caris bent to place her briefcase on the ground and gasped as it slid out of her hand. It burst open, spilling the contents on the hot tarmac.

Her cheeks burned as she grabbed for a pair of lace panties lying there like a collapsed angel. She understood now why her secretary had grinned as she'd placed a "good-luck present" in Caris's briefcase. Caris shoved the panties back in her case.

"They're in here somewhere," she mumbled, searching the variety of pockets. She'd never known her briefcase to have so many different compartments.

Her loose hair tickled her nose, sticking to her slightly perspiring face. She flung the soft strands over her shoulder with an irritated grunt. Her eyes met Alex's. She was certain hers glowed with embarrassment, his burned with amusement. And something else.

She forced her attention back to her search. "Ah. Here it is!" She pulled out her ticket with a triumphant flourish.

Alex took it from her, his touch lingering. She felt the silent connection although their fingers were separated by paper.

He looked over her shoulder and motioned behind her. She turned and was startled to see a man behind her, waiting to retrieve the luggage. She had completely lost track of her surroundings. She squared her shoulders. It wouldn't happen again.

The wind picked up, blowing her hair across her eyes and she raised her arms, attempting to replace her hair clip.

"No." Alex murmured so softly only she heard it.

"Excuse me?"

He fingered a golden lock and she shivered as though he had touched her skin. "I like your hair like that. You look beautiful."

"I'm not supposed to look beautiful," she snapped churlishly. She pulled away. "I'm a lawyer."

Alex chuckled.

She fixed her hair in jerky, irritated motions, subduing the tresses as best she could without mirror or comb.

Of all the arrogant, macho jerks, Caris thought, pulling her hair so tightly she almost yelped in protest. How typical of a man! She had spent long, hard years getting her law degree and working her way up in the legal community, yet all Alex Navarro could say when he met her was that she was beautiful! How arrogant! How infuriating!

How nice.

She nudged the reluctant admission aside, trying to ignore the feeling of instant, automatic pleasure she'd felt.

He thought she was beautiful.

The practical lawyer in her took over once again. She snapped the hair clip shut on her emotions as well as her hair.

2

"SHALL WE GO?"

Alex indicated the silver Land Cruiser parked on the dirt road that ran alongside the tarmac.

Caris glanced at the small building that served as an airport, rather desperately, he thought.

The commuter plane ride over the choppy waters of the Gulf of Mexico could be almost as nauseating as the two-hour ferry ride from Galveston, and many passengers exited the plane looking green. Alex wondered if it was motion sickness that made Caris gaze so longingly at the tiny building.

"Are you feeling all right?" he asked, softly enough so that only she would hear.

"Fine. Great. Never better." She nodded jerkily. "Let's get this over with," she muttered, and he was sure she hadn't meant to say that aloud.

Before he could comment, she turned and stalked toward the Land Cruiser, her posture as stiff and determined as a mountain climber about to attack Mount Everest. He walked behind her, enjoying the view of her rounded bottom rubbing against her gray cotton skirt before he chided himself for his uncharacteristic behavior.

She had a marvelous figure with soft, lush curves other women must envy. Curves he could well imagine in the froth of lace he'd witnessed a few moments ago. But why did she insist on hiding her femininity as though she was ashamed of it?

He shook his head. Yet another mystery for him to solve

before the next week was through. He smiled. Alex had always loved a mystery.

Harrison passed him, walking quickly, puffing heavily and trying hard to act normally. The words *power walking* came to Alex's mind.

"Perhaps Ms. Johnson should sit in the front seat."

Harrison stopped short, his hand just about to make contact with the front door of the car. Arm still outstretched, Harrison shot Caris an outraged look, and it was all Alex could do not to laugh.

"I don't mind sitting in the back," Caris said, probably reacting to the open hostility Alex could see in Harrison's gray eyes.

Harrison smiled. His lips twitched rhythmically, reminding Alex of a cat's tail.

"Allow me." Michael reached around Caris with a flirtatious wink, throwing open the back passenger door with a flourish. Alex half expected him to bow.

"I don't think so," Alex murmured. He rubbed his chin as though he was considering something. "I'd hate for Ms. Johnson to get ill from the ride." He placed his hand on the small of her back. He could feel the damp heat of her perspiring skin through her jacket.

He felt her shiver.

"The road along the coast curves and twists, and you looked ill exiting the plane." He shrugged. "Motion sickness is nothing to toy with."

He expected someone to call his bluff any moment, but no one did. Caris allowed him to lead her to the front seat, her head turned to Harrison for guidance.

"Of course, of course," Harrison said, playing the gentleman and opening the front door for her. "Ladies first."

Caris narrowed her eyes, displaying a flash of green-eyed temper and Alex swallowed his smile. Ms. Johnson, it appeared, didn't take kindly to being reminded she was a woman.

He closed the car door decisively.

Too bad.

They were on his island. *Home court rules*, he thought. He fully intended to make sure that axiom applied.

The minute he'd seen Harrison striding determinedly toward the front passenger seat, he'd known what the man was up to; he'd intended to begin discussions on the land deal while Alex was occupied with navigating the narrow, weather-roughened roads. But Alex had practically invented that negotiation tactic. There was no way he was going to allow Harrison to use it against him.

Especially not on his turf.

Alex settled into the driver's seat, consciously avoiding looking at Caris. He could feel tension vibrating from the soles of her sensible shoes to the top of her recalcitrant hair. She'd managed to put her hair back in its bun, most of it, anyway. There was still a shimmer of flyaway wisps to remind him of her femininity.

"I could have sat in the back seat," she hissed, low enough for only him to hear. "I wouldn't have minded."

"But I would have," he answered.

Her eyes widened in surprise. Whatever she had been expecting him to say, it hadn't been that.

He watched as a pink-tinged flush rose from the top of her high-collared blouse, past her smooth pearls, to the roots of her bound hair.

"I wish you wouldn't stare like that," she said curtly.

"I wasn't aware that I was staring," he said, knowing he was lying. He forced himself to look away.

She wasn't really beautiful, he reminded himself. Not classically beautiful, anyway. Her lips were too full, and her eyes—green and not blue as he'd expected—held a wariness he'd never found attractive. So why was he drawn to her as though she were the only woman he'd ever seen?

He couldn't stop looking at her.

Caris stared out the window, her toe tapping erratically in an action he guessed was unconscious.

She reminded him so much of his fellow financial analysts in New York City, the ones who made all the deals but didn't have a life outside of the office. A typical type A personality, surviving on caffeine, adrenaline and anything else they could use to make it through the day.

Although he'd run in their circles for a brief time, Alex had never fully understood those people. He always wondered when they ever had fun. Did Caris Johnson ever relax? Was there a man who knew just the right spot to massage on her shoulders so her body went limp and she leaned back, placing her head against his chest, allowing his hand to slide from her shoulder to her...

"You're doing it again!" She tapped her foot harder.

He blinked twice and felt himself flush, caught staring like a hormonal schoolboy. "I'm sorry," he murmured, realizing both Michael and Harrison were now listening to their conversation with undisguised attention.

"I realize, Mr. Navarro, that some men are uncomfortable dealing with women on an equal basis, but I would like you to try to look at me as a lawyer and deal with me on that level. I can guarantee that you'll have no problems with my work."

"Believe me, Ms. Johnson, I have no doubt about your professional abilities." *Just about my sanity.* "And please, call me Alex."

She nodded, smoothing a few stray hairs behind her ears. Her pearl stud earrings, sedate and classic, winked at him and he wondered what she would do if he removed her earrings using only his teeth.

A tap on the window caught his attention. Carlos, his best friend from grade school and the first man who'd volunteered to help him win over the Washington, D.C., lawyers, stood outside.

"I'll have the boys put the suitcases in the back."

Alex nodded. Caris and Harrison didn't need to know that the boys were Carlos's sons, pretending to be employees to make the island, and Alex, appear better off. "Thanks, Carlos."

He turned and handed the baggage receipts to Caris. Her finger brushed his palm and he felt a shiver of awareness shimmy up his spine, making him sweat although the day was cool by island standards.

What was wrong with him? He didn't even like blondes, especially not type A blondes who were tied up tighter than shrink-wrap on a new package.

"You can stop staring now!" Caris tightened her lips.

"Oh. Right." Alex looked away, trying to pretend he'd been staring at the coastline.

Caris stared at the back of Alex's head and nibbled her bottom lip miserably. She was overreacting. If she wasn't careful, she was going to blow this deal, and all because she couldn't handle life without cigarettes.

Caris balled her fingers into a fist then released her breath on a shaky sigh. She really had to have a cigarette soon. No telling what she might do otherwise.

She searched through her handbag looking for something besides her foot to put in her mouth.

"What are you looking for?" Alex asked, pulling the car onto the main road.

"Gum. Candy. Anything."

He reached into his breast pocket and pulled out a square of sugary bubble gum. "Will this do?

"Bubble gum?" She remembered buying this gum as a child, enjoying the comic in the package almost as much as the sugary concoction. "Don't you have anything a bit more adult?"

She bit her lip, trying to swallow her ill-mannered words. She'd be better off not speaking if she was going to keep insulting the man.

"It's for my eight-year-old neighbor, Christopher. He doesn't like *adult* gum."

She noticed with relief that he was smiling.

"Want it?" Alex asked again.

She shook her head. "I couldn't. It's for your neighbor." She wasn't desperate enough to steal bubble gum from a child.

Not yet, anyway.

"I've got another full bag at home. Christopher's mom made me promise to dole them out to him in small doses. Take it."

"Thanks."

The gum was as sweet as she remembered but surprisingly stiff to chew. She chewed diligently, wishing she were smoking instead. The flavor reminded her of her youth; lazy summer days in Connecticut when joy was a jump rope and a friend to play hopscotch with.

"This is really tasty."

Alex stared at her lips. The gum had left a soft dusting of sugar on her lips. He ached to lick it off, wondering if she would taste sweeter than the gum.

"What are you two talking about?" Harrison called from the back seat, sounding like a petulant child.

"Nothing much," Alex answered, pulling his attention back to his driving. "This is the main street on the island," he said, pointing around him.

"Will this take us to the resort property?" Harrison asked.

"No. We'll need to build a road."

Harrison looked aghast. "How do you get there now?"

"Using a four-wheel drive on a dirt road." Alex indicated a white building overlooking the bay. "That's the school."

"It looks small," Caris said. "How many children are on the island?"

Not enough, Alex thought, but aloud, he said, "About thirty. They all attend high school on the mainland, though.

And over there is a small maritime museum," he said, pointing again.

As he played tour guide, a role he was familiar with, Alex kept a surreptitious eye on Caris.

She sat on the edge of the seat, chewing the gum energetically. Alex wondered if she was this tense in her own surroundings. It looked as if only her seat belt and propriety kept her from jumping from the car.

He tried to imagine the island as she saw it. Tropical palms swaying gracefully on sandy shores. Fishing boats bobbing in crystalline water. Gulf breezes lending the air a fresh, salty tang.

He only hoped she wouldn't notice the way the salty air shortened the life of almost everything in its path. Cars, only a few years old, were as rusted as those abandoned in junkyards on the mainland. The houses, freshly painted in anticipation of this merger, were already beginning to fray.

If he was lucky, the merger would be signed before the whole place fell apart. Or his true financial situation was revealed. He crossed his fingers, praying his lawyer had been able to stall probate as he'd promised.

Again, Alex wondered just what Caris saw when she looked at the island. Did she pity the people their poverty or recognize that they were probably happier than she was, and definitely less stressed?

Caris leaned forward, oblivious to his speculations, the stiff seat-belt strap biting into her collarbone.

There! There was another one!

A young woman sat on a wooden porch swing puffing on a cigarette.

Her head whirled around to watch the woman smoke until she was out of sight.

Another one!

A middle-aged man, portly and slick with sweat, ground out an unfiltered cigarette with the heel of his black cowboy boot, and she couldn't stop her gasp, her fingers flying to her mouth in horror.

What a waste! There had been four more puffs at the very least.

"Are you all right?"

She jumped, having forgotten she wasn't alone. She shot Alex an irritated glance. "I'm fine..." Her voice trailed off as her attention was caught by a small grocery store advertising...

Cigarettes!

The car flew past the shop and she twisted in her seat, wishing she could go back in time and hide some cigarettes in her suitcase.

"You don't look all right," Alex said.

"I'm fine," she snapped, irritated with him and everyone else at the moment. She pasted a fake smile on her trembling lips. "I'm fine, really. Thank you."

Alex didn't appear convinced, but at least he turned his attention back to the road.

This is ridiculous, Caris thought. She couldn't think of anything but cigarettes. She'd be useless as an attorney, and she could just forget the promotion she was after. She was sabotaging her career by quitting smoking.

That settled it. She'd just have to buy a pack of cigarettes. It was either cigarettes or her career. Never mind that she'd quit cigarettes for that very same reason: her career.

Now, if she could only get to a store...

"You don't look all right," Alex repeated, breaking into her thoughts.

"What? Oh, I'm fine, really." She continued staring out the window.

"There's no shame in having motion sickness, you know," Alex continued as though he hadn't heard her. "Why don't we stop and rest for a few minutes." He pulled the car over on the road.

"Really, you don't have to go to any trouble for me. I'm fi—"

And then she saw them.

Cigarettes. Sitting on the top shelf of a rickety wooden stand, right next to bottles of beer and soda and packs of chewing gum.

She salivated, thinking of her first puff.

She was almost out of the car before the dust settled. At least she tried. Somehow her purse got tangled with the seat belt and by the time Alex came around to help her, she was swearing like a longshoreman, using words she hadn't realized she knew.

"Ms. Johnson!" Harrison gasped, staring at her as though her hair had turned purple during the flight and he was just now noticing.

"Sorry." She tightened her lips and continued to scream the words in her mind.

"Let me help you," Alex said.

She forced herself to sit still, watching Alex disentangle her from the seat belt.

He had beautiful hands. Big, capable, strong hands. You could tell a lot about a person just by looking at their hands. Bodies and faces could be camouflaged by clothing and makeup, but hands were truly the picture of a person.

She glanced down at her own hands, the manicured nails recently bitten to the nub, her inoffensive pale pink polish hanging on by sheer willpower.

If hands truly were the guide to a person's soul then she was in big trouble.

"All set," Alex said, stepping away.

She jumped down from the car and headed straight for the kiosk. "I want that," she said, pointing.

"What?" the woman behind the counter asked.

"I'd like a soda, too," Harrison said behind her. "Something cold. And not diet. Can't stand the stuff."

She froze.

The vendor pulled a dripping can of cola from a small cooler and glanced expectantly at Caris. Caris tried to devise a way to buy cigarettes without anyone seeing.

"Do you need some help?" Alex asked, standing behind her.

"Is there a problem?" Michael asked.

Does everyone need to be here watching me? she wondered irritably.

"Tell her what you want, Caris," Harrison said, the edge of a whine scraping his voice.

At that moment she hated him.

"What would you like, Caris?" Alex asked, stepping up to the counter.

She forced a smile, her lips so tight she could feel them pulse. "A cola, please."

Cigarettes! her mind screamed.

When she stepped back into the car, the cold bottle of soda dripped icy water down her skirt. She wanted to cry.

Caris was silent as the car continued along the coastline, passing fading cottages and children playing noisily in the surf.

The Land Cruiser hit a huge pothole. She dropped the unopened soda in her lap.

"Sorry," Alex said, not taking his eyes off the road. "One thing we'll need to do is fix the roads."

"That's what taxes are for," Harrison said.

"Our tax money is tied up in other things," Alex said. "Like the school and the local medical clinic."

He hit another pothole. Caris swore she could feel her internal organs reassembling.

"Make a note, Caris," Harrison said, his teeth rattling with each bump in the road. "We'll need to repair the roads as soon as possible. No tourist will put up with this, no matter how lovely the scenery."

Caris gritted her teeth to stop herself from telling Harrison she hadn't spent all those years in law school training to be a secretary.

Alex swerved to avoid what Caris considered a crater but what someone with less imagination might consider a pothole. The road conditions deteriorated the farther they drove from the airport.

"I hope you realize," Michael said in a tone that made Caris wonder what he was up to. "You're only one of many bids we're considering." He leaned forward until his upper torso was even with hers.

Caris glanced around him at Alex, wondering if this was the truth or merely a ploy to raise their bid.

"You're mistaken, Michael," Alex said, his tone calm although his hands gripped the steering wheel harder.

"No, you're mistaken, Alex."

Alex's face tightened so slightly she wondered if she had imagined it. When he twisted the steering wheel, tossing Michael into the back seat, she knew she hadn't.

"Sorry," Alex said, looking more victorious than repentant. "Pothole."

Caris felt a bubble of inspiration. There had been no large pothole for them to avoid. She had found the first hole in Alex Navarro's business empire: his brother, Michael.

ALEX PULLED the car onto the private road that led to the Navarro family compound, feeling the familiar mix of homecoming and suffocation. He glanced at Caris. Her mouth was hanging open in a caricature of awe as she stared at his ancestral home.

Alex had to admit it was an impressive sight, as long as you didn't look too closely. For behind the marble columns and sweeping vistas lay rotting staircases and plumbing problems big enough to bankrupt any small nation, let alone his barely solvent company.

"This is it," he said, stepping out of the car. The others followed.

He stood near Caris, so closely he could smell her perfume: Chanel No 5 and something else he couldn't quite decipher.

"What do you think?"

She nodded, looking like a lawyer about to tell an untruth. "It's quite nice."

She was so transparent. He couldn't resist shaking up her composure. He leaned toward her, his breath stirring the loose tendrils of hair by her ear. "Your mouth says, 'Nice,'" he whispered, "but your eyes say, 'Wow.'"

She blushed and pulled away. "Mr. Navarro, I—"

"Alex," he reminded her, enjoying teasing her more than he'd enjoyed anything in a long time.

"Alex, I—"

She froze, staring at something behind him. He turned, wondering what had overtaken her so completely.

His sister, Kate, was hiding at the side of the house. He was reminded of when his sibling was four and believed she could become invisible merely by closing her eyes.

He could smell the smoke from her forbidden cigarette and see the tip of one scuffed sneaker.

He closed his eyes. When had Kate arrived? And what was she doing here?

"Kate?"

His sister poked her head around the corner, pushing hair the same color and texture as his own out of her sad brown eyes.

"Hi, Alex. Hope you don't mind, but—" she ducked the hand holding the cigarette behind her back "—Thomas and I came for a visit."

He heard Michael click his tongue against his teeth then add, "Glad to see you finally left Paul."

Kate flashed Michael a wounded look and Alex wanted to deck his brother. Not that he disagreed with Michael. On the contrary. It was past time for Kate to leave her philandering jerk of a husband. But Michael could have been gentler—not to mention more discreet in front of their guests—and Kate's timing could have been better.

It was bad enough he had to hide the company's true financial status from one sibling. He wasn't sure he could hide it from Kate, too. Alex fought to control the panic rising inside him. If Kate and Michael found out the truth, this deal was as good as dead. And so was the island.

"Alex?" Kate's voice warbled and he smiled reassuringly.

"We'll talk about it later, Kate. Come meet our guests."

She dropped the cigarette.

"I thought you quit," he chided gently.

She flushed. "I did, until—" her gaze darted to Caris and Harrison standing behind him "—until we decided to come visit." She ground the cigarette into the dirt with the toe of her sneaker.

Out of the corner of his eye, he saw Caris flinch.

He held out his hand and when Kate put hers in his, he could feel the fine tremble no one else might have noticed. He squeezed her fingers gently in support, feeling more like her father than her brother. It wasn't a job he had requested but, like control of Navarro Investments, it was a responsibility he couldn't relinquish.

Alex pulled Kate closer to the group. "Kate, this is Harrison Peters and Caris Johnson, the two attorneys bidding on the beachfront-property partnership."

Kate held out her hand and Caris took it gently, thinking that if she squeezed too hard, Kate might break.

Caris knew very little about Kate Navarro. According to her research, Kate lived in Houston with her husband, Paul, a man with few friends and an unnatural abundance of enemies. Although Caris had only met the man on paper, she knew and despised his type. Tough, mean and willing to mow down anything in his path—including his gentle wife.

Although she knew she shouldn't take sides in this family drama, she was silently rooting for Kate to remain strong and divorce the bastard.

As Kate shyly pulled her hand back, Caris sneaked a peek at Alex. He looked unsettled. She wondered if Kate's arrival had somehow thrown Alex's plans for the merger off-kilter.

Her glance slid back to the cigarette Kate had discarded, still smoldering in the dirt. One thing was certain: at least now she knew where she could find a cigarette.

"Ah, yes," Harrison was saying, holding Kate's hand as though it were a poisonous snake. "You're the third sibling and owner of Navarro Investments."

Kate pulled away from Harrison, dug her hands into her pockets and rocked self-consciously on her heels. "Oh, I don't have anything to do with that. Alex is the financial wizard of the family. I'm just..." She shrugged as though she had no idea how to describe herself.

"Kate's just a mommy," Michael sneered.

Kate shrank back and Caris's stomach burned as it always did when someone was being bullied.

"I've heard being a mother is the hardest job anyone can ever have," Caris said.

Kate shot her a tremulous smile. "You'll like the beach, Caris. Maybe you'll have a chance to get a tan and relax."

"Unlike some people, she has a job to do," Michael said and Kate blushed, once again shriveling into uncertainty.

"I know that, I just meant—"

Alex placed a hand on Kate's arm, reminding Caris of a medieval knight protecting his queen. "Of course there will be some time to relax. You know what they say, Michael. All work and no play..."

Michael snorted. "Funny, brother, but that is one thing I thought you would never say to me."

Alex narrowed his eyes, his nostrils flaring in a valiant attempt to remain calm. He turned to his sister, his soft voice conveying nothing of the anger Caris suspected was bubbling under the surface. "Where's Thomas?"

"John took him over to Christopher's house to play," Kate

said. "And I was meaning to ask you about that, Alex. Why's John here? I thought he was working in Galv—"

"So Thomas is with Christopher?" Alex interrupted, his voice rising. He tugged his sister away from the group. "That might not be a good idea."

Kate frowned. "Why not? Thomas and Christopher always play together."

"Christopher just got over chicken pox," Alex said.

"That's odd. Barbara never mentioned it."

"Maybe you'd better go get him."

"That's okay." Kate waved away Alex's concern. "Thomas had chicken pox last year."

"Actually, it was mumps," Alex said. "Or maybe measles."

Kate stared at her brother. "Chicken pox? Mumps? Or measles?"

Alex shrugged. "One of them. Why don't you go get him, just in case."

Kate looked confused but she nodded. "All right. I hope to see you all at dinner."

"Of course, Kate." Alex grinned, looking more relaxed. "You're as much a part of this deal as I am."

Michael muttered something under his breath and Alex's face changed again, sending a chill up Caris's spine. Alex looked lethal, his tanned skin stretched into a grimace, his eyes colder than anything else in this tropical climate.

He looked dangerous, and she found herself drawn to him so completely it frightened her.

3

As THEY STEPPED inside the mansion, Caris didn't even try to hide her astonishment. The foyer alone was larger than her entire Washington, D.C., apartment. She tipped her head back, staring at the vaulted ceiling, and squinted. Was that a water spot she saw?

Harrison whistled softly behind her, the sound teetering between reverence and rudeness. "Is that a Monet?" He peered closely at the painting, one hand poised as though to touch it.

"My sister, Kate, painted it," Alex said. "She's an artist."

"She's very good." Caris stepped back from the impressionistic painting noticing as she did that the painted wall immediately surrounding the picture was a much brighter white than the rest of the wall. Apparently, in the past, a different, even larger painting had hung there.

"Your compound appears quite extensive," Harrison said. "How many acres do you have?"

"Three acres on this site, but we own about two hundred acres on the rest of the island."

Two hundred and forty-seven acres, to be precise, Caris thought.

"I'm eager to see the property we'll be purchasing," Harrison said. "Your prospectus indicated it was several hours' drive from here. I'd like to leave for the property tonight."

Harrison's comment sounded much more like a demand than a request, and Caris wasn't surprised when Alex looked offended.

But it was her job to make sure Alex Navarro didn't get offended. She recalled her abysmal behavior in the car and winced. She'd have to take control of herself.

"I'm not telling you to baby-sit Harrison," Martin Joffrey, another senior partner at the firm, had advised Caris in a private meeting yesterday. "But Harrison has a habit of steamrolling his way through life. I want you to make sure he doesn't steamroll his way right out of this deal."

"You're putting me in an awkward position," Caris said. "In advising Mr. Peters, I run the risk of offending him..."

"And ruining your chances of making partner in this firm as long as Harrison has a voice in the selection of new partners," Joffrey finished for her. "I understand that, but I never said you had to work through Harrison Peters."

"Excuse me?"

Joffrey winked at her and she felt her stomach plummet, straight to the bottom of her sensible shoes. "Alex Navarro is a handsome man. I'm sure that if you think about it, you'll have no problem finding a solution to your problem."

"You're not suggesting I..." She couldn't finish the sentence without feeling nauseated.

"No, no, of course not. That would be setting myself up for a sexual harassment suit, now, wouldn't it?" He smiled at her. "What I mean to say is that I'm sure you'll find a way to ensure we close the deal without offending either Harrison or Alex Navarro." He cocked his bald head at her. "Do we understand each other?"

She was still too numb to feel anything but amazement that she had spent most of her life developing her brain, yet the only thing men seemed to notice about her was her body.

She had no intention of following through on Joffrey's unspoken plans, but she did intend to do whatever she had to to stop Harrison from pushing their firm right out of this deal.

And herself right out of a partnership.

"You're frowning, Caris. Do you disagree?"

She whirled to face Harrison. "I'm sorry, what did you say?"

Harrison sighed, his thin face pinched with disapproval. "Daydreaming, I suppose."

"No, I..."

"Harrison and I were discussing our travel plans," Alex said. "How would you feel about leaving tomorrow for the beach?"

Caris felt her mouth go dry. She wasn't going anywhere until she got some cigarettes, and especially not to a deserted beach town where she'd be lucky enough to find a bottle of mineral water, let alone a cigarette.

"Well, I—"

"It's settled, then." Harrison's eyes barely swept over her and Caris tried not to get annoyed. Harrison was the senior member on this trip, and therefore the one making the decisions, but she couldn't help feeling dismissed.

"We don't have to leave tomorrow." Alex stared at her, his brown-eyed gaze intense. Usually, when anyone gazed at Caris so unblinkingly, she felt like a legal clause in a codicil—to be taken out, picked apart and thrown back in some haphazard fashion. But today, with Alex gazing at her, she only felt warm and most surprisingly, cared for.

She shivered. Odd that he affected her so strongly. Must be the cigarettes.

"Tomorrow will be fine," Caris said.

"Of course it will be fine," Harrison said, sounding surprised that there had even been any question about it. "Tomorrow. At the crack of dawn."

Alex forced a slight smile. "We'll leave at 9:00 a.m."

"But—" Harrison sputtered.

"It's only a two-hour drive to the beach."

Harrison might be foolish enough to argue. Caris, fearing defeat before negotiations even started, glanced around, seeking something to distract Harrison. "Is that a Picasso?" She pointed down the hall.

"They're quite valuable," Harrison said, moving as quickly as a bloodhound chasing down a new scent.

Alex chuckled. "I can see why you two are partners."

Caris stiffened. "Why?" Didn't he think she could handle this on her own?

Alex's smile faded at her brusque tone and Caris felt like kicking herself. Alex had only been making conversation and here she was, jumping down his throat.

She smiled weakly. "Sorry. It must be jet lag making me act like this." More likely, the cigarettes, but she wasn't about to tell him that. "What were you going to say?"

"Just that you provide a good foil for Harrison's negotiating style."

Or lack thereof, Caris thought. Harrison reminded her of a grizzly bear defending his territory by challenging everything that came into sight—even butterflies.

"Harrison seems to view any compromise as defeat, whereas you appear to understand the art of negotiation," Alex said.

That might have been a compliment, but years of working in a male-dominated field made Caris wary. "You're not implying that I can't play hardball, are you? Because I have to tell you, I'm very good at it."

Alex's lips quirked in an increasingly familiar smile. "I'm sure you're good at anything you set your mind to."

Caris was annoyed to feel herself glowing with pleasure. Why was he being so nice to her? And why was she soaking up his attention as eagerly as a water-starved flower?

"It seems to me," Alex continued, "that you understand when hardball won't work and when a bit of finesse is required instead. I'll let you in on a secret." Alex leaned closer, his musky scent making her feel light-headed. "Hardball only makes me hit back. Harder."

Alex pulled away and Caris took a deep breath, surprised to find she'd been holding her breath. She could still smell him, still feel his presence around her as comforting as a warm blanket yet as disturbing as a Stephen King novel.

She shook her head, trying to chase away the strange path her thoughts had taken. Caris was the queen of tough negotiations, yet here she was, thinking about a man's cologne.

Cigarettes. She wasn't willing to attribute her reactions to anything else.

Alex watched the thoughts whir in Caris's head. Had he been too blunt, warning her off like that? Harrison would probably have taken his words as a challenge, but Alex hoped his impression of Caris was correct. That she was the calmer member of the team, the brains behind this merger. If he was right and she handled the negotiations with a soft touch, this deal might work out.

If he was wrong, he'd just signed the island's death warrant.

Alex glanced down the hall. Harrison was leaning close to Kate's Picasso-like painting, running his finger along the edge of the refurbished frame. Panic bubbled in Alex's belly. Behind the painting lay a hole bigger than his four-year-old nephew, Thomas. His meager budget had allowed only minor touch-ups to the ailing property. He couldn't afford to repair the house's many structural problems, like the caved-in section of the wall obscured by Kate's painting, and had merely hidden them, hoping the house wouldn't fall down before the deal was secure.

"Why don't I have someone show you to your rooms?" Alex hoped he didn't sound as desperate as he felt. He moved backward and collided with John.

"You rang, sir," John said in full British accent and Alex suppressed a wince. John had promised he'd play this role straight. No accents, no gimmicks, just a straight, boring butler for a rich guy trying to plan a merger. Alex turned around, expecting the worst, and got it.

John's costume—a gray tuxedo complete with white cotton gloves—must have come from his last job, dinner theater in Gainesville where he'd played a Jeeves-like butler in a British comedy.

Alex wished he could have hired a real butler and not coerce his friend into acting like one. "John, please show Ms. Johnson and Mr. Peters to their rooms."

John clicked his heels together. "Certainly, sir. If you'll follow me, please, Ms. Johnson."

Alex sneaked a look at his guests. Caris looked amused, not surprising considering John's real forte was comedy, not drama. But Harrison looked impressed, which was exactly what Alex had been aiming for.

"The dinner party will begin in three hours," Alex said. "I'll send someone for you."

As they walked away, Alex heard Caris ask, "Did anyone ever tell you that you look like Jeeves, the butler in those old British movies?"

"Jeeves who?" John asked, never cracking a smile.

Alex heard Caris's laugh long after she had disappeared from view. He turned away with a smile and came face-to-face with Michael.

"How long have you been here?" Alex had assumed Michael had gone to his room. He was unsettled by the impression that his brother had been spying on him.

"Long enough," Michael said. "Could I talk to you for a moment?"

It was the last thing Alex wanted, but he couldn't refuse. Not if he wanted Michael's cooperation with this merger. "Sure. Let's go into my office."

They turned down the hallway and entered the study Alex had appropriated for his home office. Unlike the rest of the house, this room was in top shape, having been the first and last room renovated before Alex discovered that the once-wealthy Navarro Investments was on the verge of bankruptcy.

Alex sank into the leather chair he'd brought from his apartment in New York and waited until Michael settled onto the matching leather sofa. "So, what's on your mind?" Alex asked. "Whatever it is, you can tell me." Alex wondered if Michael's playboy past had finally caught up with him and he was about to become a father. Again.

Michael stood. "I need a drink. Want one?"

"No, but you go right ahead."

Michael walked over to the hand-carved mahogany cupboard, another appropriation from Alex's New York apartment, and filled a shot glass with Johnnie Walker Black. Michael drained it, placed the glass back on the bar then filled it again.

"Whatever it is, Michael, it's probably easier if you just tell me," Alex said.

"It's about this morning."

Alex waited until Michael sat back on the couch, a third full shot glass in his hand. "Yes. Go on."

"I wanted to apologize for this morning, the thing with the Japanese. You were right. I crossed the line. I'd like to make it up to you."

Warning bells clanged in Alex's mind. "Oh?"

"I'd like to go with you to the beach, perhaps help with the sale."

Alex doubted that his brother wanted to help. More than likely he was looking for more holes in Alex's cover story. But Alex knew it would be easier to keep an eye on Michael at the beach rather than leaving him alone in town to interrogate the locals. "We're leaving tomorrow at nine. Kate will be coming, too."

Michael frowned. "Does she have to come?"

"Kate is a full partner in Navarro Investments, just like you and me, Michael. So, yes, she *has* to come." Plus, she needed the break. Alex could tell by the glazed look in her eyes that she was reeling from her impulsive flight from her husband. Alex didn't want her running back to Paul in a weak moment. At least if she was with them at the beach, he'd be able to offer her support if her newfound courage wobbled.

"She's not bringing the kid, is she?"

Alex sighed, knowing his idea of family and Michael's were radically different. "Thomas is a child, Michael. Not a piece of furniture you can conveniently leave behind."

"The neighbors could keep an eye on him," Michael said. "I mean, Thomas spent the whole day there, anyway."

Alex frowned, feeling what little patience he had with his brother disappear. "Thomas is coming with us. Kate will keep an eye on him."

"Kate can barely keep an eye on herself," Michael muttered.

Alex glared at his brother.

"So, is John coming, too?" Michael asked in a deceptively casual tone.

The hairs on the back of Alex's neck stood at attention. He fought not to fidget. "Of course John is coming. He'll be doing the cooking." John was also an integral part of Alex's plan, but unfortunately, Alex couldn't tell his brother that.

"It's sad really," Michael said.

"What?"

"John. He had such a promising future in acting."

He still did. But Alex couldn't tell his brother that, either.

"Still, everyone knows the theater isn't a reliable career." Michael shrugged. "Even for someone with a modicum of talent."

Clenching his fist beneath the desk, Alex bit back the urge to defend his friend. "Are you coming with us or not?"

Michael drained his glass. "Of course. Someone has to look out for my interests in Navarro Investments."

"What the hell does that mean?"

"You figure it out."

"Michael—"

But Michael had disappeared, leaving Alex to wonder

when his family had crumbled as completely as a child's sand castle at high tide.

There was a knock on his door and Alex's head shot up. Kate stood in the doorway, chewing her bottom lip nervously. He stifled a groan. He couldn't take much more.

"Kate—"

"I've left Paul," she blurted out.

He nodded. "I know."

She stepped into the room, pulling the door shut behind her. "I knew he was cheating on me, and I told myself it didn't matter. I loved him once, and I swore I'd never raise my child alone but..." She sank onto the couch, her earlier defiance fading. "One day, it just got to be too much." She raised her gaze to his and he ached to see tears in her eyes. "You know what he said when I left?"

Alex sat next to her. "What?" He took her hand in his. It was cold and he squeezed her hand softly, wishing life had been easier for his beloved younger sister.

"He told me to go. Just go." She snorted indelicately. "He threw me away, just like that."

"Oh, Kate—"

She raised her angry gaze to him. "And he had the nerve to tell me I'd never get a penny from him if I left. That he'd keep the case in court until Thomas was out of college and on his own. You know what I told him?"

His stomach tightened. He had a feeling he knew what she'd told him.

"I told him he could stick his money you know where. I don't need his money."

She tossed her head and Alex winced.

"It's okay, isn't it, Alex?" Her defiant tone shriveled into uncertainty. "I mean, the last time I checked, Navarro Investments was doing really well."

Alex fought to keep his expression blank. Navarro Investments hadn't been doing well for a while now. But Kate obviously didn't know that.

"Alex?"

"Of course it's fine, Kate. Navarro Investments is doing fine." His tongue tripped lightly over the last word, but luckily Kate didn't notice.

"Good." She tried to grin, but Alex saw through the facade. "I'm glad I have you to help me."

She sank back against the couch and closed her eyes wearily.

Alex rubbed her hand. "Anything you need, Kate, I'll get it for you." No matter what he had to do.

She squeezed his fingers, then sat up. "Lots of changes going on. What's John doing working for you? Last I heard, he was working on a show in Galveston. There was even talk of him taking a job on Broadway."

"Talk?" He arched one eyebrow and a glimmer of satisfaction warmed him as Kate blushed.

"I do keep in touch with some of the old gang. They keep me up-to-date on everyone."

And especially on John. Alex remembered when it hadn't been at all clear who Kate would marry—Paul or John. He'd always thought she chose the wrong man. Now he knew for sure.

"John and I are helping each other out," Alex said. "For now."

"And what about this deal?"

Alex tried not to flinch. "What about it?"

"We don't need the money, do we? I mean, we're not in any danger of going broke, are we?"

He could see the wheels spinning in her head, and fear expanded over the deceptively brave expression on her face. "We're doing fine." He patted her hand. "Believe me."

"Good, because, if we weren't, I could get some money from Paul." She gulped. "Somehow."

He knew what she would do. Go back to the bastard. Not if he had any say in it. "Don't you worry about that, Kate. Everything's going to be fine. I'll take care of you."

"But the deal?"

"It's just another business deal. You know I've always wanted to provide more jobs to the island."

"Yes, but what happened to all the furniture?" She lowered her voice. "The house is almost empty. And so rundown. Do you know there's a hole in the wall of my closet the size of a cow?"

He tried to look surprised. "I haven't really had the time to deal with housing repairs, what with Dad's funeral and all."

Kate flushed. "I'm sorry. I should have helped with that. It's just, I was busy dealing with Paul, and..."

And like Michael and Alex, Kate had no love for their father.

"It's all right, Kate. I took care of it." Just as he took care of everything else.

Kate nodded.

"Do you need anything?"

She shook her head, then paused. "Well, actually..."

"Yes?"

He watched a rosy blush slide up her cheeks. "You didn't hide my cigarettes, did you? I mean, I know you hate it when I smoke, but you didn't take them, did you?"

"No, I didn't."

"John," they both said.

Kate sighed. "I'll have a talk with him and see if I can get him to hand them over. It really annoys me when he tries to take care of me like this." But she didn't look annoyed. She stood. "Can I come to the beach house with you?"

"Of course." He stood beside her. "I assumed you were coming."

"Well, I..."

"What, Kate?"

She flushed. "Michael doesn't want me there."

He grasped her hand. "But I do. And—" he paused "—so does John."

"John?" Her expression brightened.

"Someone has to keep him company while I negotiate this deal."

"I could do that. If it would help."

He tried not to grin. "It would be a big help, Kate."

"Nine o'clock, then."

They were both smiling as she turned away.

CARIS EYED HERSELF critically in the full-length bedroom mirror.

This will not do. I look like a junior judge. And a male one, at that.

She ripped off her pantsuit in disgust. Hadn't she packed one outfit that didn't make her look like a clone of Harrison J. Peters III?

She scattered her clothes on the bed, noticing that if you discounted the frilly underwear and the business skirts, everything else could belong to Harrison J. Peters, Esquire, or any of the other male attorneys at her firm.

She swore softly.

However she looked, she had to stay on her toes. This merger was her shot at making partner. And she wasn't going to let some ex–financial analyst ruin it for her. Even if he was a rich, educated and sexy ex–financial analyst.

A surge of inadequacy shot through Caris, making her knees wobble. She needed to get the upper hand, and soon, or this deal would be over before final negotiations had even started. On the other hand, if Alex had been telling the truth, she'd be foolish to push ahead in pseudo-Harrison style. She'd only anger him, and destroy any chances of a successful deal. Besides, feeling as nicotine-deprived as she did, she'd fall flat on her face if she tried a show of strength. Caris felt too off balance to negotiate a grocery list, let alone a million-dollar merger. She needed to even things out, somehow. Keep Alex Navarro off balance long enough for her to get a cigarette and return to normal.

She looked at her wardrobe again. She couldn't do that with the clothing she'd brought.

For once, she wished she had something that would make a man forget she was a lawyer and remember that she was a woman with needs and desires just like any other woman. She wished she'd brought the red dress she'd never worn out of her apartment.

She shook her head, laughing, and turned to the window to look out at the tropical scene. Where had that come from? For the last eight years she'd been doing everything she could to subdue her femininity. Now tonight she wanted to flaunt it?

Cigarettes.

The familiar craving came out of nowhere. Her skull pounded to a Latin beat and she wondered if she had time to find Kate and plead for a pack of cigarettes.

Hell, the way she felt now, she'd better ask for an entire carton.

She looked back at the clothing on the bed. For the first time since law school, she wasn't interested in dressing as all the dress-for-success books recommended.

Instead, she wanted someone to say "Wow" when she entered the room.

She sank onto the bed. Who was she kidding? She didn't care about the rest of them.

She wanted Alex to say "Wow" when she entered the room.

She was restless, filled with almost forgotten emotions that undulated like a living creature inside her. She hadn't felt this way in years, at least since college.

He thought she was beautiful.

She felt as though a thousand ball bearings were rolling around inside her, touching off sparks and shorting out circuits.

She shook her head. She was acting ridiculous. She'd be fine as soon as she had a cigarette.

But she didn't believe it.

She paced the large room, her eyes following the paths of sunlight decorating the white marble floor.

She clenched her fists. Get a grip, she told herself. She'd spent far too many years working her way toward partner to sabotage herself with her own emotions. *Act like the lawyer you want to be,* she told herself, instead of the woman you once were.

Caris had always been different, even as a child. When all the other little girls played house, Caris played war with the boys. At first they didn't want her to play, but after she won most of the battles using her intellect and very few soldiers, she was the most popular general on the block.

In her early teens, the boys wanted her again. This time it wasn't for her intellectual skills but for her budding breasts, blond hair and long legs.

Caris could never understand why the same boys she had discussed strategy and kill tactics with now refused to discuss anything more serious than high-school dances and getting to first base.

But it wasn't until her first year of law school that Caris discovered how much of a detriment her attractiveness and femininity could be.

She had applied for a summer internship at a prestigious law firm in New Haven, Connecticut, a few miles from her dorm. Everyone knew she was going to get the job. After all, there was no one more intelligent, no one more eager to succeed, and no one with better grades.

She was more confused than devastated when she discovered the internship had been given to someone else.

"Why wasn't I chosen?" she asked her only female professor, Lenore Davidson.

Professor Davidson appeared to consider her answer carefully, which surprised Caris because she was one of the few professors in the conservative law school who always had a quick answer.

"Caris, it was felt..." She cleared her throat. "How can I say this? They thought..."

"They thought what?"

Professor Davidson stacked and unstacked the papers on her desk as reluctantly as a parent about to tell a child their dog was dead. "The selection committee thought someone else might make better use of the internship."

Caris blinked rapidly and sat back in her chair. "What? I don't understand."

Professor Davidson shook her head. "They chose Bradley Summers."

Caris frowned. Bradley Summers was a classmate at Yale. While intelligent, Bradley was no match for Caris. "Why? Does his father play golf with the managing partner or something?"

"Have a seat, Caris. I don't quite know how to tell you this."

The leather chair squeaked as Caris sat, mimicking the nervousness skittering inside her. "Just tell me the truth."

Professor Davidson took a deep breath. "Internships at prestigious law firms are designed to expedite the training of lawyers."

"I know that. That's why I applied."

"You're a beautiful woman, Caris."

"So? Bradley Summers is pretty cute, too. What does that have to do with my not getting the internship?"

"Most beautiful women get married and have children. And after the children come..."

"Wait a minute." Caris sat up straighter. "Are you saying they gave my internship to someone else because they thought I might get married and not be a good lawyer? That's illegal!" She could cite the cases, too. "I could sue them!"

"You need proof, Caris."

"I have proof."

Professor Davidson smiled sadly. "No. You don't."

"But, you just told me..."

Professor Davidson shook her head, her short gray hair swinging softly. "Hearsay, Caris. When I learned they hadn't picked you for the internship, I was extremely surprised. You're the best student I've ever had and I think you're going to be an incredible lawyer."

"The selection committee obviously didn't agree."

"No, they didn't. And I couldn't imagine why anyone would pick Bradley Summers over you, so I called a friend at the firm and asked him point-blank."

"And...?" Caris prompted.

"They said you were too pretty. Pretty women do not make good lawyers."

"That's not true!"

Professor Davidson tapped her pencil against the desk in rhythm with Caris's frustration. "I know that, Caris, but most of the law firms in the United States are run by men, usually older men who still believe that a woman can't have it all—beauty *and* brains."

"But that's so unfair."

"I know, Caris. I wish the world was different but it's not. It's trite but true, this is still a man's world and if you want to succeed in it, you're going to have to adapt to men's standards."

Caris stared at her adviser knowing that whatever she decided today would affect the rest of her life.

"When people look at you... No, when *men* look at you," Professor Davidson said, "they see a beautiful woman. Not an intelligent future lawyer, not even a dedicated student. They see beauty. Period. Most people won't look further than that. It's a sad fact, but the more attractive a woman is, the less intelligent she is expected to be. Just look at yourself."

Caris glanced down at her denim skirt and red cotton top.

"You look like a woman," Professor Davidson said.

Caris's laugh was stilted. "I am a woman."

"Question is, do you want to be a woman, or do you want to be a lawyer?"

"Can't I be both?"

"I haven't found it to be possible, but maybe you'll be one of the exceptions."

Caris had trusted her instincts too long not to know that Professor Davidson was telling her the truth.

In order to get what she wanted, she would have to subdue her feminine side and choose logic over passion. In other words, she had to act like every other male law student and lawyer she had ever met.

The first thing Caris changed was her physical appearance. She donated her sandals and cotton skirts to a women's shelter and replaced them with sensible shoes and business suits.

She couldn't make herself cut her hair, which she considered her only truly attractive feature, so she did the next best thing. She hid it. Hair combs, bobby pins and buns became her allies, camouflaging the feminine beauty that would stop her from achieving her goals.

She gave her makeup and costume jewelry to the women in her study groups, keeping only the pearl necklace her family had given her when she graduated from high school.

She hid her feminine side from the world and indulged it only in ways that couldn't be seen. Caris probably had the most extensive lingerie collection in all of the greater Washington, D.C., area. Too bad no one else had ever seen it. For it had been years since Caris had been with a man in anything but an intellectual manner. She couldn't remember the last time she had looked at a man and imagined kissing him.

And she never looked at a man and wondered what it would be like to touch him, to lie naked next to his hard, hot body.

On the contrary, when she looked at a man, she wondered what it would be like to *be* him; free to act as she wished, to dress as she wished, and to know she would be accepted for the person she was.

But today everything had changed.

Today, when she had looked at Alex Navarro, she hadn't wondered what it would be like to be him.

She had wondered what it would be like to be *with* him, in every way a man and a woman could be together.

Caris shook her head. Of course, that would never do. She was here to do a job and Alex Navarro was no more than an adversary, a man she hoped to influence in the boardroom, not the bedroom.

Maybe later, after the job is done...?

Caris shook herself mentally, refusing to tantalize herself with things that would never be, and turned to the clothing on the bed.

She dressed in the business suit that had always made her feel powerful, and went in search of the dining room, her emotions once again as controlled as her hairstyle.

4

ALEX TAPPED his fingers against the mantelpiece. Where the hell was Caris Johnson?

The teenage housemaid-in-training he'd sent to fetch Caris hadn't been able to locate her. A search of the property had turned up nothing but John and Kate kissing furtively in one of the darkened hallways, and Michael doing his best to interrogate the youthful servants.

Where was she?

More important, what was she doing?

Was she snooping, discovering the empty rooms where the antique furniture had been auctioned off to pay some of his father's more immediate debts? Maybe she'd fallen through a rotting floorboard and was able to view the devastation of his homestead from a more unique angle?

Whatever Caris was doing, she wasn't here.

And as for John, he should be annoyed with his friend. After all, John was here to supervise the inexperienced wait staff, helping to convince Harrison and Caris that Navarro Investments was still a force to be reckoned with. He wasn't supposed to be mooning after Kate like a lovesick teenager.

But Alex didn't really mind. It was worth personally supervising the preparation of tonight's dinner, even teaching the young waiter how to serve soup from the large tureen, just to see Kate's cheeks flushed with pleasure, her eyes sparkling with renewed youth.

He glanced at Michael, and his smile faded. Too bad his brother didn't have a flirtation to keep him occupied.

Alex narrowed his eyes. If he didn't know better, he'd suspect Michael was here to sabotage the deal. But weren't they on the same side? And he still didn't understand why Michael wasn't in school. He might have a deserved reputation for being a party animal and a flirt, but he did take his education seriously. So why would he leave during finals?

The sight of Harrison wandering between the small groups of dinner guests caught Alex's eye. The lawyer was none-too-surreptitiously casing the dining room. What would he do if he discovered the true state of the Navarro household?

Alex glanced at the ceiling, praying it wouldn't leak during dinner. They only had to get through tonight. Tomorrow, he'd whisk everyone away to the beach house which, miraculously, had been renovated only a year ago and was still in good shape.

He needed Caris and Harrison to believe that he was rich enough to choose his business partners, rather than desperate enough to accept any offer.

Where was Caris? He had no doubt she was searching for any information she could use to influence the deal. Servants often provided a wealth of information for those daring enough to seek it out.

Alex suppressed a chuckle. Caris wouldn't find out anything, especially not from his so-called staff. They were all volunteers, most barely out of high school. He'd promised them a job at the resort if they helped him clinch this deal. The only information these volunteers could provide was how poorly they were trained.

The hairs on the back of Alex's neck rose suddenly, as though a bolt of lightning had barely missed him, sizzling the ground beneath him. Caris had just entered the room. He took a deep breath, steeling himself for the sweet thrill he couldn't control.

Caris lingered in the doorway, dressed in an olive business suit and matching low-heeled pumps. She looked every inch the controlled attorney in spite of the uneasiness he could see in her green eyes. She had redone her hair; her bun was so tight he wondered if it was cutting off the circulation in her scalp.

Without stepping from the corner where he was eyeing the borrowed Ming vase, Harrison said, "Glad you could join us, Caris." The chill in the man's voice was blatant.

"I got lost."

Although Caris hid her hands inside the roomy pockets of her blazer, Alex could see two lumps and knew they were clenched in twin fists.

How was it possible Caris looked more tense after a three-hour rest than when she had first exited the plane?

CARIS CHEWED on her lower lip miserably.

I can't believe I couldn't find one cigarette on this entire compound!

She had been scouring the house and grounds for almost three hours, looking for Kate and her precious cigarettes.

The first housemaid she encountered had been friendly when Caris smiled and claimed to be lost. Two hours and six employees later, they weren't as trusting and Caris was given a personal escort to the dining room.

Still without a cigarette!

Now she stood in front of a group of obviously wealthy and powerful strangers who stared at her as though she'd wandered into the wrong dinner party. She wished she could disappear.

"Would you care for a glass of wine before dinner?" Alex asked, standing by her side.

She jumped slightly, unnerved that he had managed to cross the room without her being aware of it.

"I'm sorry. I didn't mean to startle you."

"You didn't." Her voice was higher than she intended, and when she smiled, a nerve in her right eyelid twitched. She reached for the glass of white wine he held and took two quick sips. "Thank you."

He smiled oddly at her and she had the feeling he'd asked her a question and was waiting for a response.

"What?" she asked, still on edge from her fruitless search for nicotine.

"That was my wine."

She looked at her glass. It had only been half-full when she took it from him. She had taken her host's drink and practically drained it. "I'm sorry. Here."

She tried to give him back the glass, but Alex chuckled and said, "Keep it. I'll pour myself another."

The butler, John, whom she privately referred to as "The American Jeeves," scurried toward her, a full glass of wine in one hand, a newly opened bottle in the other.

John shot an apologetic glance toward Alex then asked Caris, "Would you care for more wine?"

"Yes. Thank you." She held out the almost-empty glass and watched as he poured it, twirling the bottle so expertly it didn't dare drip.

With a polite nod, John left. "Where did you find him?" Caris murmured.

Alex's lips twitched. "Here on the island. Why?"

Caris shrugged. "Doesn't he remind you of one of those British butlers from the movies?"

Alex glanced at John, who was now passing around a silver tray of hors d'oeuvres, a look of polite disdain on his controlled features. "John has a keen theatrical sense."

A female giggled huskily and Caris turned to see a stunning woman staring at them from across the room. She looked like a beauty queen. All she was missing was a sash and a diamond tiara. Caris shivered, wishing she was wearing her sexy red dress. At least then, when people stared at her, she would know why they were staring.

"I hope you're hungry," Alex said. "We held dinner for you." His hand hovered over the small of her back. Although he never touched her, she could feel the heat of his fingers through two layers of clothing.

While he led her to the table, she wondered if she would see a burn mark when she undressed tonight.

"Where's Kate?" Caris asked as she settled into the seat on Alex's right.

"She's...resting." He hesitated over the final word and she wondered what else he was hiding from her. "In addition, her son, Thomas, is sick."

"What's wrong with him?"

"He has asthma, and he's having trouble breathing tonight. She's staying with him to make sure he rests like he's supposed to." Alex took his place at the head of the table.

At his slight nod, John escorted a young man barely out of boyhood into the room. The boy carried a large ceramic soup tureen so tightly his knuckles were white. It looked as though any movement might send the hot soup tumbling into a guest's lap.

Caris looked away, unable to watch the boy's too-careful actions. "Kate's son has asthma?" Caris asked. "That's so sad. Will he be all right?"

Alex offered her a roll from a small basket then placed one on his own plate before nodding. "He's resting comfortably now. Thank you. That's one of the reasons I was so upset with Kate earlier."

"Upset?"

"The doctors have told her it's not healthy for Thomas to be around cigarette smoke, yet Kate started smoking again. And as I've reminded her, it's not good for her health, either." He emitted a frustrated sound. "So many people die from smoking. If I had my way, I'd declare the whole practice illegal."

Caris told herself she shouldn't get angry, but she did, anyway. "So you'd regulate everyone's life? What about alcohol? Alcohol probably causes more deaths than cigarettes. Would you raid weddings and throw anyone drinking a champagne toast into jail?"

The table fell silent. Caris realized her comment had been too antagonistic.

And far too loud.

"I had no idea you were such a proponent of hands-off government," Harrison said, turning away from the silver candlesticks he'd been eyeing.

She stared at her soup bowl, wishing she could hide behind the soup's steam curtain. "Normally, I'm not," she murmured.

"What?" Harrison asked, his voice rising. "We can't hear you now, Caris."

She raised her head feeling defiant, though outnumbered. "I said, normally I don't do this."

"You don't normally speak your mind?" Alex asked. "Or you're normally more tactful about it?"

His smile told her he was enjoying their exchange. One glance at Harrison's slitted eyes told her Harrison wasn't.

Caris shrugged and placed all of her attention on the bowl in front of her.

"I'm glad you like the soup," Alex said softly, as soon as the other conversations had resumed.

"It's very good." If he asked her what flavor the soup was, though, she'd be lost.

The dinner passed much too slowly for Caris. Although John was efficient, the rest of the serving staff appeared to be overly cautious, almost as though this was the first meal they had ever served. When dessert and strong black coffee were finally brought out, Caris pleaded exhaustion and headed for her room.

"We'll leave for the beach at nine tomorrow morning," Alex reminded her. "Sleep well."

Alex watched Caris scurry from the dining room.

If he hadn't known better, he would think someone was chasing her.

"Don't tell me you're falling for the little lawyer," Michael said, his voice close to Alex's ears.

Alex swallowed his coffee, wishing he knew what had turned the brother who used to adore him into his enemy.

"Like fine music and beautiful artwork, Caris Johnson is a pleasure to behold."

"Funny," Michael said, sipping his brandy, "but neither of the pleasures you mentioned involve touch. And brother, we both know beautiful women are meant to be touched."

With a nod, Michael sauntered toward the woman who'd been eyeing Alex earlier and set about seducing her.

Alex turned his own eyes toward some business associates from the mainland and felt nothing but disdain. The combined income in this room could settle the national debt of most countries, not to mention his small island, but, aside from John, his pretend butler, there wasn't one person here he felt comfortable enough to call a friend.

He'd invited the crowd knowing Harrison Peters would be impressed, and perhaps a little intimidated. Alex was merely playing by Harvard rules. Those who appear the strongest win, no matter what.

Alex had expected Caris to be impressed and to spend the evening hobnobbing and politicking with the wealthy guests, as Harrison was doing. Instead, she had left the dining room as though a pack of hungry hyenas were after her.

He sipped his coffee, still thinking of Caris. Perhaps, like fine music and fabulous artwork, there was much more to her than the surface suggested.

He glanced around the room one last time then put his coffee down. It suddenly tasted as bitter as the company he kept. Without a backward glance, he left his own party, knowing no one would miss him.

His footsteps were silent in the darkened night as he retreated to his bedroom. Burning with frustration, Alex stripped. He left a path of clothes lying across the moon-dappled floor and slipped into his bikini swim briefs, his muscles aching to burn some of the stress he'd felt building the entire evening.

He hurried to the pool, cracked but still functional, and dived in. His body barely rippled the surface. He swam methodical laps, feeling his frustration evaporate as his muscles warmed.

He swam silently, hoping to exhaust the demons that shadowed him. Demons that taunted he would always be alone.

CARIS PACED in her darkened bedroom, waiting for the dinner party to end and the rest of the house to fall asleep. She glanced at her watch again, biding her time until she could continue her search for a cigarette.

She suspected Alex had told the servants to keep an eye on her, especially after today's foray through the compound, but, she reasoned, even servants had to sleep sometime. Especially servants who appeared so young and inexperienced. In the meantime, all she had to do was wait.

She didn't blame Alex for not trusting her. If she were in his shoes, she wouldn't trust herself, either. For all he knew, she had been searching the compound for incriminating or conflicting information that would affect the land sale, scouting for messy half truths she could hold over Alex Navarro's head.

She stifled a mirthless laugh.

Truth be told, she hadn't thought about the deal in hours.

All she could think of was cigarettes.

And Alex.

She stopped suddenly, surprised by the revelation, but it was true. She'd been thinking about Alex, running over the memory of him like a much-loved photograph.

She shook her head and resumed her pacing.

She'd better get a grip on herself. If she didn't watch it, she'd soon be writing him love poems and doodling their combined names all over her legal briefs.

A splash outside caught her attention and she hurried to the window.

Alex dived under the water, his body shimmering beneath the underwater lighting. She feasted on the sight of his strokes devouring the length of the pool.

He was magnificent, his body dark and lean, his masculine power contained only by a small black swimsuit.

She couldn't stop the unconscious groan that slid past her lips, but she tried, pressing her trembling, half-chewed fingernails against her mouth.

Alex must have sensed her gaze because he turned and floated on his back. She stepped back into the shadows of her room.

He stared at her open window while he performed a lazy backstroke just for her. He smiled, his teeth a gleaming white against his darkened face, and showed off smooth muscles that would make a bodybuilder jealous.

His gaze never left her window.

She backed away, her hands still against her mouth, willing no further sounds to betray her.

She sank onto the bed and glanced at her watch again. It was too soon to go exploring, and she wasn't sure which of the many bedrooms belonged to Alex Navarro.

It wouldn't do to run into him in the hallway, him wearing his minuscule swimsuit, dripping water and male sensuality while she wore a guilty expression, an expression she used to be able to camouflage before she quit smoking.

And before she met Alex Navarro.

"I'll sleep for a little while." She leaned back against the bed. "Then I'll look for a cigarette."

Her eyes closed and she slept.

WARM WATERS of a crystal clear lagoon caressed Caris's skin as soft as a lover. Tension eased out of her as steadily as a retreating tide.

Suddenly, he was there.

He took her hand and she floated into his embrace. They stayed

*together, bodies touching, lazily drifting in the water. She stared
into his brown eyes and thought, This is where I'm supposed to be.*

The man leaned closer and whispered, "I want you."

She caught her breath as his hair-roughened leg slid between
hers, his caress a sweet friction.

"Yes."

The water whispered over them, softer than a sea breeze. She
wanted to be closer to him, needed to feel him around her, enveloping her, inside her.

She took his face in her hands, pulling him closer, needing his
touch, needing his kiss.

His mouth moved tantalizingly closer to her own.

"Yes," she whispered, but still he didn't kiss her.

His mouth skimmed over her forehead. She closed her eyes and
held on to him. The world began to slowly swirl around her.

His lips trailed a sensual path to her cheeks, his breath teasing
her eyelashes. Her lips parted, waiting for his kiss, waiting.

"Kiss me," she murmured.

She felt his chuckle heat the inner curve of her ear.

"Please..."

"Soon."

While he tasted her ear with the softness of his tongue, his hands
roamed freely, creating a river of shimmering sensation. She
groaned when his hand dipped to her belly, his caress softer than
the patter of rain.

A waterfall of glimmering, shimmering, pulsating beams of light
washed over her.

But she needed more. Her fingers skimmed through the coarse
softness of his hair as she pulled him closer. "I need you."

"I need you even more." His mouth moved tantalizingly closer
to her own.

"Now."

His breath washed over her, and she inhaled his salty scent eagerly.

"Kiss me."

CARIS AWOKE with a start, unsure where she was. The room was black except for a sliver of moonlight penetrating the gap in the curtains. The curtains wafted as a slight breeze came through the open window. It was cool enough to make her shiver.

She stood, rubbing her hands over her goose-bumped arms.

The pool was empty now, the pool lights off. From her window she could see that the lights of the small town had been shut off. It looked as though someone had flipped one giant switch.

She remembered the old joke about small towns rolling their sidewalks up after 8:00 p.m. Apparently, in the case of Navarro Island, it was no joke.

It was quiet and she wondered what had woken her up.

It had been a sound, almost a groan.

She felt herself flush as she realized the groan had come from her own lips. She burned, remembering what had prompted that groan.

Caris glanced at her watch. It was almost 2:00 a.m. She must have been exhausted to sleep so soundly.

Of course, with a dream like that playing in her head, who would want to wake up?

She slipped on the shoes that she had kicked off during her sleep, and rearranged her clothing, trying not to look as though she had slept in them.

She opened the bedroom door, wincing as it squeaked in the still house. When no angry servants appeared, she took a deep breath, walked quietly down the stairs and tiptoed toward the kitchen. Floorboards creaked loudly beneath her feet and Caris froze. Was it her imagination, or did the floor feel unstable? Caris hurried toward the kitchen.

The big kitchen was silent and lonely at this late hour, the giant appliances surprisingly old for all Navarro's wealth. After searching fruitlessly through every cupboard and drawer for a cigarette, Caris settled on a chocolate bar she found hidden in the back of the industrial-size refrigerator. As a child, she had believed chocolate could cure all aches.

Hopefully, it would help this one.

With the sweet chocolate still dissolving in her mouth, her feet whispered their way down the hall.

She heard voices in the dining room and melted into the shadows, wondering how she could make it back to her room without being discovered.

If she did get caught, she had no excuse she could use. She couldn't say she was lost. She had used that one just this afternoon.

A woman laughed, and through the slit of the opened door Caris could see the beautiful woman from dinner standing in the darkened room, her hands reaching forward, beckoning someone.

A man glided into view, slipping into the woman's embrace. It was too dark to see his face. Caris squinted, trying to make out his features in the dim, yellow light. The woman laughed again, a brittle trill, and the man whispered something, his familiar voice low and deep, the words indecipherable.

As the door closed, Caris heard the soft rustle of clothing and a low-voiced moan that needed no translation.

Caris shot back up the hall, and ran upstairs to her room, sick to her stomach.

She lay huddled on the bed, the unfinished chocolate bar forgotten on the nightstand, her fingers trembling with more than cold.

Alex and the beauty queen were lovers. She should have guessed from the blatant looks the woman had been shooting him all through dinner.

Caris felt like a fool for imagining there was any reason besides business that Alex Navarro had been attentive to her. Alex had flirted with her and made her feel special in an attempt to influence the business deal...period.

Normally, she would admire his cool business head and the fact that he was willing to do anything for the deal.

Normally, she would try to emulate him, view him as a man to admire.

But not tonight. Tonight, she felt ill.

It's probably the cigarette thing making me so sensitive, she told herself.

But she wasn't convinced.

ALEX GAZED at the cloudless blue sky with a smile. It was a beautiful day for a drive.

"Where the hell is Caris?" Harrison squinted at his watch, ignoring the clear blue sky. "I'm sorry, Alex. I warned her to be on time."

Alex shrugged. "We're in no hurry, Harrison."

Michael drifted out the front door, the lovely Laura—still clad in last evening's party gown—on his arm.

"I must say, Alex," Harrison said in an amused undertone, "your brother certainly has a way with the ladies."

"Yes," Alex said, a slight twist to his mouth. *If he used half his charm in the business arena that he uses in the bedroom, he'd have more power and money than he ever accused me of possessing.*

Michael kissed Laura with a lazy indulgence Alex knew his brother had spent years perfecting. With a wave she drove away in her Mercedes, the music of the Rolling Stones ringing through the dense, tropical countryside.

Michael walked toward them, running a practiced hand through his hair in an offhanded style. "Except for being a little sleep deprived," Michael said, "I'm ready to go."

"Well, we're not," Alex said. "We're still waiting for Caris."

"And Kate." Michael glanced around. "Where is my darling sister and her little monster?"

Alex frowned. "I wish you wouldn't call Thomas that. He'll think you mean it."

"I do. Listen, do you mind if I go on ahead? The last time I took a car trip with Kate, Thomas got sick all over me."

Alex nodded, trying to hide the satisfaction in his eyes. "If you like. Why don't you take Harrison with you?"

Michael touched Harrison's elbow. "Ready, Harrison? I hope you like music."

Harrison followed Michael toward the red Toyota truck parked in the driveway. "Of course I like music. Bach, Beethoven…"

"Def Leppard?" Michael asked as they climbed into the truck. "Better buckle up, Harrison," Michael said as he gunned the engine. "Some people say I drive a little too fast."

The last image Alex had was of a stricken Harrison, hanging on to the door frame for dear life as Michael pulled out of the driveway in his usual manner: too hard, too fast and with total disregard for the people left behind in clouds of dust.

Alex smiled. He couldn't have planned this better had he tried. Alex knew Kate and Thomas wouldn't be driving to the beach until later today. But of course, Michael didn't know that.

"I thought they'd never leave," John said, thankfully without his fake British accent. He lowered his voice. "Michael cornered me last night to console me on my failed acting career."

Alex felt his blood chill. Michael had never consoled anyone in his life. "What did you tell him?"

"That I was upset but managing. And of course grateful to my best friend, Alex, for providing me with a salary until I could land another job on stage."

Alex tried not to grin. He suspected John had shed a few fake tears. "And he bought it?"

"Of course." John looked properly horrified. "I am the best actor on Navarro Island, after all."

Alex grasped his friend's hand. "And the best friend a man could ask for."

For once, John looked flustered. "That's what friends are for, Alex. So—" he cleared his throat "—is Kate really back for good?"

Even John, the best actor on Navarro Island, couldn't hide the plaintive yearning in his voice.

"That's what she said. She left Paul."

"About time." John grinned. "I always knew she was a smart lady. So—" he kept on grinning "—want me to play butler and fetch the pretty lady lawyer for you?"

Alex grinned back. "Thanks, John, but there's no hurry. I can wait."

5

CARIS COULD PRACTICALLY hear her future partnership with Harrison, Harrison, Joffrey and Peters disintegrating as she flew down the main staircase at 9:28 a.m., nearly a full half hour late. Time was money in the world of law—literally, as the firm billed by the hour. Her firm was more intolerant of tardiness than most. They'd fired their last paralegal for being five minutes late.

Lord only knew what Harrison would do to her.

"I'm so sorry I'm late!" Water from her sodden ponytail dripped down the back of her shirt. She had been in such a panic when she'd woken late that, after a quick shower, she'd barely had time to restrain her hair in a ponytail, let alone its usual bun.

Alex was smiling at her. He looked far too relaxed and she frowned.

"Did I get the time change wrong? Is it nine-thirty or seven-thirty?"

"It's nine-thirty."

"I overslept," she said, wondering why he wasn't angry. "Where is everyone?"

"Michael drove Harrison to the beach."

"I can't believe they didn't wait for me."

Alex laughed, taking the small suitcase she was carrying from her fingers. "Believe me, you're not missing much."

He placed the suitcase in the back of the car, next to his cellular phone.

"I'm really sorry I'm late." She realized she was wringing her hands and forcibly stopped the apologetic action. "I must have been more tired than I realized from yesterday's flight." *Or last night's 2:00 a.m. meander around the house.*

"I'm not sorry," Alex said. "As a matter of fact, I should thank you. I wasn't looking forward to a two-hour ride with Harrison and his constant politicking. As for Michael..." He avoided her gaze, which made her think he wasn't about to confide the entire truth. "Well, Michael can be difficult for me to take even in small doses. Two hours in a closed space could prove lethal."

Alex's smile deepened, his teeth flashing white against his tan. "Come on. Let's go."

"What about Kate and her son?"

"They'll be driving up with John later."

"So it's just us?"

He grinned and she suspected he had planned it that way. "It's just us."

Why did that worry her?

As they drove away from the house, the view of the coastline was even more spectacular than it had been yesterday. Probably because she wasn't consumed with thoughts of cigarettes.

Funny, but she hadn't thought about smoking in at least five minutes. Maybe the edge was wearing off.

"What's your preference?" Alex asked.

She didn't know what he was talking about until she noticed the compact discs in the case lying between the two seats.

"You can choose. I'm not particular." Caris rarely listened to music, used it only as background noise while she accomplished something else, like exercising or compiling a legal brief.

"Pick something," Alex said. "Once we leave the town, we won't be able to pick up any radio signals."

She rummaged through the large, eclectic collection and picked Vivaldi's *Four Seasons.*

Violins filled the car.

"I wouldn't have pegged you for a Vivaldi fan," Alex said.

She bristled, wondering if he could see the lack of cultural stimulation in her childhood. The closest she'd ever gotten to classical music as a child had been a scratchy record of Prokofiev's *Peter and the Wolf*, narrated by some actor from the 1950s. "Why? I thought everyone liked Vivaldi."

"That wasn't meant as an insult." He gave her an indecipherable look.

"Then what did you mean it as?"

"When I look at you," he said, looking only at the road and not her, "I'm reminded of Rachmaninoff. All passion and energy."

Caris felt the base of her skull tingle. The first time she'd heard Rachmaninoff during her collegiate search for cultural knowledge, she'd felt a strange kinship with the impassioned pianos and sharp-edged harmonies. But she'd subdued her preference, assuming the classical strains of Vivaldi's violins would better suit her life as a successful and refined attorney.

"No offense was intended," Alex said. "It was just a comment."

A very astute comment.

She looked out the window, unsure what to say.

"Which road is this?" Caris asked as they pulled away from the town.

Alex chuckled. "The only road. The only paved road, anyway. But we can change all that once we begin building the resort."

Caris wished she had the nerve to begin negotiating the land deal, but all her research showed Alex Navarro negotiated on his timetable. They would begin negotiations when he was ready, and not before. It would be foolish to risk alienating him simply because she was impatient.

After the Vivaldi CD finished, Caris put in Rachmaninoff. Her pulse leaped as the second concert filled her body.

"I thought so," Alex said with a small smile.

Caris was surprised to find herself relaxing during the ride, even though parts of the paved road were barely better than a dirt path in some places. As they traveled along the coastline, she stared longingly at the pristine beaches and whitecapped water until she reminded herself she was here to work and not to frolic in the surf.

Unbidden, an image from last night's erotic dream flashed into her mind. She glanced sideways at Alex. She'd woken before his lips had touched hers. Would his kiss have been softly seductive or masterfully demanding? And then she recalled the scene with Laura, and felt ill all over again.

"Are you all right?" Alex asked.

"W-what?"

"You were staring at me. Are you feeling carsick?"

Caris felt herself blush hotly. "No. No. I'm fine." She stared out the window.

"You look hot."

She whirled on him. "Excuse me?"

"You look overheated. Would you like me to turn up the air conditioner?"

Caris laughed shakily. "Really, Alex. I'm fine." She fanned herself with a sweaty hand. "Maybe you should turn up the air conditioner. Just for a few minutes."

By the time Alex pulled the car onto a small, pitted road and drove toward the ocean, Caris was feeling more like herself.

"Is this it?" They'd only been on the road an hour. She'd thought the resort area was farther than that.

"No. This is Corazon Inlet. I thought we could stop and stretch our legs. Unless you don't want to."

"No, that's all right. We can stop." Caris wanted to get to the beach house before any more images of a wet and naked Alex flashed disturbingly in her mind, but she knew when to be polite.

She gritted her teeth as the Land Cruiser bounced through potholes almost as tall as she was. Finally, Alex pulled up to a whitewashed building that sat at the apex of the inlet. Behind it, the gulf gleamed a pure and tranquil blue.

"This is beautiful," Caris said, her love of the water overtaking her nervousness.

"I'm glad you like it. It's my favorite place on the island." Alex stepped out of the car. "Are you hungry?"

"A little." Caris hadn't eaten anything since last night's pilfered chocolate bar. This morning, all she'd had was a cup of strong coffee one of the housemaids had brought to her room.

"Good. Follow me." Alex led Caris through the small building and onto a wide outdoor patio overlooking the inlet.

They settled on a wooden picnic table. Caris kept her gaze on the shimmering water.

The waitress, a rotund woman of Native American descent, hurried toward them. As she walked, she wiped her hands on an apron that had once been white. When she smiled, Caris could see huge gaps where her teeth had once been. "Mr. Alex!" She pumped Alex's hand energetically.

"Hello, Maria." He turned to Caris. "I hope you like fish. It's a local specialty."

Caris's stomach growled. "Sounds great."

The woman left, smiling broadly.

"You must be famous," Caris said, her fingers fiddling with the salt and pepper shakers. "Everyone seems to know you."

"It's a small island." Alex looked out at the water. "Why don't we take a walk."

"What about our food?"

"It'll be a while." Alex stood and held out his hand.

Caris knocked over the saltshaker, unnerved by the thought of being so very alone with Alex.

Her mind flashed to the honeymooners she'd seen on the plane. Were they walking on a beach hand in hand? Making love in the warm, tropical currents? Or staying in their hotel room, existing on a steady diet of room service and love?

"We should wait here," Caris said. "It doesn't take long to cook fish."

Alex winked at her. "They have to catch it first."

She thought he was kidding until she saw Maria walking toward the water with a bucket.

"That'll take forever!"

Alex shrugged. "Life moves at a slower pace on Navarro Island." He held out his hand once more. When she didn't move, he added, "Fish tastes better fresh."

"I'd still prefer to wait here." Caris crossed her arms and planted her feet firmly on the wooden floor.

Alex's smile faded. "I consider this inlet a part of our partnership deal and I'd like to show it to you."

Caris knew when to accept defeat, but she'd never learned to accept it gracefully. With a sigh, she stood, ignoring Alex's smile and his still-outstretched hand.

Alex dropped his hand and said, "Follow me."

AS THEY DESCENDED the rocky path toward the beach, Alex could feel the tension radiating from Caris.

He'd never met a more anxious woman. For a moment in the car, he'd felt her relax and had hoped they were entering a new phase of their relationship. But then she'd tensed again and they'd been back to square one.

A loose rock skittered under his foot and Alex held his hand out to Caris. "Be careful. It's a little steep here."

Caris ignored his hand. "I'm fine, thank you, I... Oh!"

Pebbles scattered along the path, taking Caris with them. She slid into him, and where they touched, Alex tingled. He tightened his hands around her waist and forced a note of polite concern on to the roughened edges of his voice. "You okay?"

"Yes." She stepped back carefully. Her gaze landed on the shimmering water and she took a deep breath. A ghost of a smile skimmed the edges of her lips, transforming her. She closed her eyes and lifted her face toward the sky.

She was the most beautiful thing he'd ever seen.

"Caris?" He'd think she was hurt if she didn't look so happy.

When they opened, Caris's green eyes sparkled with sunlight and joy. She took another deep breath and grinned. "Can't you smell that?"

His senses barely registered the tang of the salty air; all his concentration was focused on the vibrant woman in front of him.

Caris laughed. "Isn't this glorious?"

"Yes." But he wasn't thinking about the salty air.

She stood before him, a sensual creature aglow with pleasure. He wanted to kiss her, he wanted to touch her, he wanted to make her forget about the coastline and think only of him.

Caris turned toward him. Gone was the shrouded, suspicious lawyer who had intrigued him. In her place was a sea nymph, a woman full of life. Full of joy. Full of love.

Caris held her arms out and twirled. He held on, not because he was afraid she was going to fall, but because he needed to touch her.

"Caris..." His voice was rough and he tightened his hands.

Caris giggled. "Last one to the beach is a rotten egg!"

She pulled away from him and raced down the rocky path. Alex followed at a slower pace, his gaze never leaving her.

He watched her kick off her shoes and bury her toes in the sand. He liked this side of her. He liked it very much.

He walked toward her. "I see you like my favorite place."

Caris turned to him, her eyes lit with laughter and the sparkle he'd always known was there. "There's something about the water that just makes me feel good."

He was feeling pretty good himself. "You are an amazing woman, Caris."

She blinked, startled. "I am?"

He took a step toward her. "You are."

He felt her tremble as he placed a tender hand on her cheek. She was soft, her skin warmed by the sun and cooled by the gulf breezes. She licked her lips, and he ached to kiss her there, but first...

Alex reached behind her head and tugged her ponytail free. "There, that's better," he said, fanning the soft, golden tresses around her in the loose, carefree way he'd seen in his dreams. "Now you look like the water nymph you are."

She smiled shyly at him. "Alex, I..."

He waited, but she didn't continue. Her green-eyed gaze, once so nervous and scattered, moved to his mouth and stayed there.

Alex's chest tightened. If he didn't kiss her soon, he was going to explode.

Purposely taking his time, Alex placed his lips on her forehead. He felt Caris shudder against him, her soft sigh teasing his neck.

"Alex," she moaned, lifting her face for his kiss.

Although his body ached to possess her lips, his instinct told him to go slowly—to worship every inch of Caris, and then start all over again, just for the joy of it.

He slid his lips over the soft down of her cheek, absorbing the scent of her, perfumed as she was by gulf breezes.

"Alex, please." She startled him, placing her hand on the back of his neck and pulling him closer, her mouth seeking and finding his.

With a jolt of pleasure, Alex realized he'd finally come home.

Caris opened her mouth under his, seeking him, inviting him. His hands slid down her back, reveling in the soft friction of skin and cotton. He grasped her hips, tugging her closer, sensing he would never get enough of this woman.

"Caris..."

She moaned in response, offering herself blindly to his touch.

He bent his head to her ear, wanting to say everything yet not knowing how to begin.

"Caris, love."

It took only a second for his words to sink in. Alex cursed the impetuous tongue that had uttered those words. He felt Caris stiffen, felt the water nymph transform back into a controlled lawyer. When she pulled away, he groaned.

"Caris, don't."

She ran shaky hands through her hair. "Where's my ponytail holder?" She searched the sand. "And where are my shoes?"

"We need to talk about this," he said.

Caris's gaze skittered over the sand as she looked for the pieces of her wardrobe that he sensed would make her feel like a lawyer again.

"I need my shoes."

He bent and handed them to her, saddened by the knowledge that he'd lost something very precious.

"Thank you." Her tone was stiff, her body even stiffer as she visibly strove not to touch him.

"Caris, we should talk," he repeated.

"No. We shouldn't." She ducked her head, still searching for her ponytail holder.

He reached into his pocket and rubbed the elastic hair accessory absently.

"Have you seen my ponytail holder?" She sounded as though she was skimming the edge of panic.

He fingered the elastic again. If he gave it to her, she'd pull her hair back and become Caris Johnson, attorney-at-law, and he didn't want that.

He left the elastic in his pocket. "No, I haven't. Caris, we need to talk."

She tightened her hands into tiny fists, her eyes blazing

righteous fury. "I can't blame you for what happened here, Alex. I was just as much in the wrong."

A surge of unexpected anger rose in Alex. "What happened here wasn't wrong, Caris."

"Maybe not to you," she said. "But it was disastrously wrong for me." She shook her head, self-recrimination creating worry lines on her face. "I have no excuse for what happened. None."

"You don't need an excuse," Alex said. "Why are you looking at this like it's a bad thing? Passion like this doesn't happen every day."

"Passion like this shouldn't happen!" Her face softened, making her appear more desperate than angry. "Alex, this shouldn't have happened. Not between us."

"Then between whom?" Alex asked. "You can't choose who you're going to lo—" He broke off, realizing what he'd been about to say.

Caris narrowed her eyes. "What were you going to say?"

"Nothing." Alex bit his lip to keep from saying any more.

He wasn't in love with Caris Johnson. He couldn't be. It was lust, pure and simple. Lord knew, he'd felt it often enough, especially in his youth.

But it had never felt like this.

He'd never had a craving to pull a woman into his arms and keep her there for all eternity. Never wanted to crawl inside another person's skin, just to understand how better to please her. Never wanted to wake up every morning staring at the same beautiful face, watching it transform over time.

It's not love! His stomach tightened and fluttered. *Nerves.*

Panic was more like it.

What had he gotten himself into?

"You're right," Alex said. "We don't need to talk about this."

Caris looked surprised, but she nodded eagerly. "Good."

"Mr. Alex!"

They looked up to see Maria waving from the porch. "Your fish is ready."

Saved by lunch.

"Let me help you up the path..." Alex turned to Caris but she was already halfway up the sand dune, racing as though the devil himself were chasing her.

And maybe, in Caris's eyes, he was.

LUNCH WAS SUPERB, or so Caris had told Alex. In truth, she hadn't even tasted the succulent fish. She'd been more concerned with stilling her shaking body and calming the hormonal surges that were still in control of it.

What a kiss! Her dream was merely a pale imitation of what had actually occurred.

Her body warmed, remembering the feel of Alex's hands against her scalp, his fingers caressing her hair so tenderly she was glad she'd never cut it short.

She twitched in her seat at the wooden table, her body responding to the memory almost as fully as she had responded to the kiss.

She sneaked a glance at Alex. If it was any consolation, he appeared as affected by their embrace as she was. His fingers nervously drummed the table and his body was in constant motion, as though he couldn't contain the tension inside him. His expression, carefully guarded from her gaze, held a mixture of shock, awe and confusion.

If she hadn't been so affected emotionally and physically herself, she might have felt some pleasure knowing that for once she seemed to be in a position of power.

God, she needed a cigarette.

Caris chewed miserably on her bottom lip, wishing she were kissing Alex instead.

"Excuse me, Alex." Maria smiled apologetically at Caris, then bent to whisper something in Alex's ear.

He frowned. "Would you excuse me, Caris? I need to take

care of something. It shouldn't take more than fifteen
minutes."

Caris nodded, needing some time to think things through.
"Take your time. I think I'll take a walk."

His mouth dropped open as though he was about to say
something else, but then he nodded and hurried away, the
older woman chattering at his heels.

Caris walked nervously toward the parking lot, knowing
she couldn't walk to the water again without obsessing over
their embrace.

Her hair bounced against her neck with each step she took.
It was surprisingly freeing to have her hair unrestrained, and
despite her craving for a cigarette and her uneasy feeling
about Alex, Caris was relaxed.

Cigarettes.

She stared at the cigarettes behind the glass case in the entryway of the restaurant, wondering if they were a mirage.
Although they didn't have her brand, Caris tapped on the
glass to gain the teenage salesgirl's attention. "I'd like a pack
of cigarettes, please."

She practically salivated, imagining the taste of her first
cigarette in two days.

The girl was slow. Caris, impatient to find a safe place to
smoke before Alex returned, threw a five-dollar bill at the
young woman, grabbed the cigarettes and a pack of matches
and ran.

She hurried past the parking lot into a grove of palm trees,
slipping occasionally on the wet grass. Safely behind a tree,
Caris unwrapped the cigarettes, her fingers shaking with anticipation.

"Miss! Miss!"

Caris hid the cigarettes behind her back, her heart beating
a guilty rhythm.

It was the teenage salesgirl. "You forgot your change."

Caris shoved the change in her pocket. "Thanks." *Now, go
away.*

She didn't have much time before Alex returned.

The girl left.

"Finally," Caris muttered, digging into the cigarette pack.

The cigarette in her lips felt like a homecoming and Caris sighed, savoring the feeling. She struck a match, hearing the magical pop, then inhaled gratefully.

She began to cough almost immediately. Her throat ached from the feel of the smoke reversing, but she persevered, willing herself to stop coughing.

After a few puffs, she felt light-headed and nauseated and her fingertips tingled. She leaned against the tree, hoping she wouldn't disgrace herself by passing out.

She inhaled again, cautiously, then stubbed out the cigarette when her head started to ache. She felt like crying as she stared at the crushed cigarette impressed in the dirt.

She had waited so long for this cigarette and she hadn't enjoyed it at all. In two days, she'd been changed from a diehard smoker into a woman who couldn't handle nicotine. It was so unfair.

She heard Alex calling her name and rubbed her eyes, which were still watering from the smoke. "I'm coming," she yelled, stuffing the cigarettes into her purse. She pulled out a stick of spearmint gum for camouflage.

The moment Caris stepped from behind the tree, Alex thought she looked different. Her eyes were reddened and she was chewing on one fingernail absently. He wondered what had made her hide behind a tree instead of taking one of the scenic walking paths along the water.

When she came closer he sniffed cautiously, smelling cigarette smoke. And the overpowering scent of spearmint.

Caris was vigorously chewing a stick of gum. Alex remembered that Kate always chewed gum after smoking one of her forbidden cigarettes. He guessed it was one of the myths smokers hung on to, that no one would notice the smell of smoke if they chewed enough gum.

Caris Johnson was a smoker.

He felt a tingle of discovery. He now knew something about Caris that she didn't want everyone to know. At the same time, he was saddened that she smoked and saddened that she hadn't trusted him enough to confide in him.

But why should she? They were merely business associates, despite that passionate kiss. Business associates on different sides of the conference table.

He couldn't explain why that distinction bothered him so much.

Caris loped up beside him, chewing her gum fiercely. "Is everything all taken care of?"

"Almost." He'd spent the last fifteen minutes reassuring the restaurant staff that they weren't going to lose their livelihoods when the resort was built. The way Alex had it planned, the restaurant would have even more business. Maria had been frightened of losing the place entirely. Apparently someone had started a rumor that a Japanese firm, Nakashimi, would be buying land on the coastline and fencing off access to the inlet. And he had a good idea who that someone was.

When he got to the beach house, he and Michael were going to have a talk.

"What will happen to the inlet when the resort is built?" Caris asked as they drove away from the restaurant.

"I'd like to provide a free shuttle bus twice a day, as well as provide rental canoes and fishing poles."

"Nice," Caris murmured. "So the guests won't get just the gulf but a quiet inlet also. It could work."

Alex beamed. He'd known they were on the same wavelength the moment he met her.

"We would need to provide food and probably an inn, so that guests wanting to stay at the inlet could," she said. "Of course, we'll tear down the existing buildings."

Alex frowned. That wasn't in his plan at all. "I've promised Maria and her staff that they can stay."

"Sure they can stay," Caris said. "We'll need workers for our restaurant."

Maria and her husband were more than mere workers. "I don't think you understand—"

But Caris was on a roll. "We could put up a four-star gourmet restaurant on one end and a burgers-and-fries kind of place on the other end. Provide a service for both aspects of the tourist population."

"There's nothing wrong with the restaurant that's there now."

Caris turned to him as though she'd just noticed him. "Honestly—" she rolled her eyes "—did you see how filthy that woman's apron was?"

Alex, who knew that Maria's other job was helping her husband in his woodworking shop in back, had never minded Maria's dirty apron. But apparently, Caris did.

"And not everyone likes fish," Caris said.

"So we'll add more to the menu."

"It's not just the menu," Caris said. "It's everything. The service was slow, the rest rooms filthy and the salesgirl in the shop moved like a senior citizen. No one will stand for having to wait to buy a pack of gum or a candy bar."

"How did you know about the salesgirl in the shop?"

Caris blinked rapidly, reminding him of a startled child about to tell a fib. "I bought some gum." She fidgeted nervously with her seat-belt strap.

And probably some cigarettes, but she obviously didn't want him to know about that. "All right, so we'll revamp the entire business. Train the staff and rebuild the restaurant. But that takes money."

Caris waved the comment away, looking more confident than she had a moment ago. "The profits from the restaurant will more than make up for the renovations."

"But what about now? Maria and Tim don't have that kind of money lying around."

"Maria and Tim?" Caris asked.

"The owners of the restaurant."

"Oh, we'll buy them out. Didn't I mention that?"

Alex tightened his jaw. "No. You didn't mention that." He'd been wrong about Caris Johnson. They weren't on the same wavelength at all. "I think there's been a misunderstanding. I have no intention of buying anyone out."

"You won't need to buy anyone out. We'll take care of that."

"Caris, you don't understand."

"Don't worry about the money," Caris said.

Alex frowned. "I'm not worried about the money. I'm worried about Maria and Tim."

Caris sighed. "Alex, be reasonable. Maria and Tim probably don't know the first thing about running a four-star restaurant, or even a burger shop. They wouldn't even know where to start."

"So we'll teach them."

Caris shook her head and turned to look out the window. "I don't think so."

Alex slammed on the brakes, wishing yet again he had the money to build the resort on his own. Caris flashed him a quick, startled look; she was on the verge of being frightened, and he felt a momentary surge of guilt for scaring her. "Didn't anyone in your firm read my proposal?"

"Proposal?" Caris asked blankly.

Alex swore and leaned his head tiredly against the steering wheel. Just as he'd feared; they weren't interested in forming a partnership designed to save the island as well as make everyone a tidy profit. They wanted to do it all themselves, their own way, without any regard for the islanders and their fragile lives.

"This isn't a problem we can't solve," Caris said. "I'm sure we can work out something about the restaurant."

"Maria and Tim stay," Alex said bluntly.

Caris considered it for a moment. "No guarantees, but I'll see what we can do."

"They stay or we have no deal."

Caris gazed incredulously at him. "Let me get this straight? You're willing to blow a million-dollar merger just because of a waitress and some guy named Tim?"

Alex clenched his fingers into a fist. "Yes."

"But why?"

Alex swore under his breath. "You don't know what it's like to live from hand to mouth, from paycheck to paycheck, never knowing if you'll have work tomorrow, or food on the table. Having to decide between a home you love or a well-paying job thousands of miles away. You were probably born having it all, never knowing what it's like to not even be able to envision what having it all looks like."

"Look who's talking," Caris said. "Last I heard, you Navarros had more money than God."

Not anymore, Alex wanted to say. He slowed his breathing, knowing he had revealed more than he should.

Since his father's death and his move back to Navarro Island, Alex's emotions had been raging as fiercely as those of any hormonal teenager's. And since that combustively powerful kiss he and Caris had shared, he was a powder keg, just waiting to explode.

He relaxed his jaw, a slight smile curving the edge of his lips as he remembered her last comment. "Last I heard, God still has lots more money than we do."

"It was just an analogy," Caris muttered.

"Albeit an inaccurate one."

She giggled, then quickly clapped her hand over her mouth as though the sound surprised her.

"I'm really sorry." She nibbled on her smile as if she was trying to subdue it. "You seem to bring out the worst in me."

"Funny," he mused, aching to kiss those lips again, "but you seem to bring out the best in me."

Their gazes met and locked. Blood pumped through Alex's veins, making him light-headed.

He had to kiss her. He just had to.

"Wait!" Caris held out her hand.

"What?"

"We're not going to do that again," Caris said. She folded her arms protectively in front of her.

"Right." Alex gritted his teeth and gripped the steering wheel, torn between wanting to touch Caris, and knowing she was right. "We're not going to do that again."

It was going to be a long drive.

6

"IT'S ABOUT TIME you two got here!"

Harrison stood in the driveway, his arms folded across his bony chest, his finger tapping an irritated rhythm on his arm as he stared at Caris and Alex. Harrison had removed his suit jacket and traded his long-sleeved shirt for a short-sleeved cotton shirt in a small concession to the high heat and humidity of the coast, and he looked angry enough to burst into flames.

Caris stepped out of the Land Cruiser, feeling as though she were sixteen again and returning home hours after her curfew.

"Sorry." Alex tossed the car keys to an awkwardly teenage male servant. "We stopped for a bite to eat on the way."

Harrison sniffed disdainfully. "Caris, really, we came here to work, not to take a vacation."

Caris opened her mouth in protest.

"I was the one who wanted to stop," Alex said. "Have we kept you waiting long?"

"No, no, of course not," Harrison stammered, shifting his feet as though he were juggling his ill-spoken words. "I just assumed that since Caris, like most women, loves to sit back and relax, she made you stop."

Alex raised one eyebrow. "It doesn't appear to me that Caris loves to sit back and relax, as you put it. As a matter of fact, she was simply being polite by obliging me."

Harrison smiled and Caris itched to slap the insincere grin from his face. "She must have been on her best behavior."

"Of course," she responded, wishing Harrison would stop

speaking about her as if she were a mute child. She turned away from Harrison, afraid she might do something completely unprofessional. Like punch him.

"He's gone," Alex said after a moment, a chuckle in his voice.

She shivered, feeling the heat of his breath curl around the sensitive skin of her earlobe. "What?"

"Harrison. He's gone." He closed her car door and led her toward the large house. "Have you and Harrison ever worked together before?"

"No. Why?"

"No reason. I just get the impression he doesn't know you very well. It was obvious to me you were only going along with my wishes."

She felt strangely pleased. "It was pleasant to stop." Her mind lingered on their more than pleasant kiss.

He smiled at her. "You make it sound as though it normally isn't pleasant to stop."

Once again, Alex seemed to see through her polite responses to the real meaning behind her words. "My mother never understood the pleasure of getting from point A to point B without making a million stops. Family car trips were unbearable. Do you know, we once took a three-hour detour to go to an amusement park for toddlers?"

"What was wrong with that?"

"We were all teenagers!"

Alex chuckled as they strolled up the brick walkway.

"My sister, Susan, loved those road trips, but as soon as I was old enough, I begged my parents to leave me home."

"Must have been lonely," Alex said.

"Not really," Caris said, realizing for the first time that he was right. "I spent a lot of time at the library."

"The library can't make up for family."

She hadn't known that then, but now, suddenly, she did. "I was first in my class until college. All that time in the library paid off."

Alex opened the front door of the beach house. "And when you went to college?"

She wasn't surprised he'd picked up on that. "I had a hard time adjusting," she said, remembering the parties and dates that had seemed more important at the time than getting her degree. "Then I adjusted." And stopped doing anything except what would get her ahead in her chosen field.

She stepped inside the house. "Wow!"

Her eyes took in everything at once: the marble floors in the entryway shone as brightly as the skating rink where she had taken lessons the winter she was nine. The staircase curled toward the ceiling like cigarette smoke, supported by solid wooden beams.

"This is your beach house?"

Alex rocked on his heels, hands in the pockets of his khaki pants, the slight smile on his face telling her he enjoyed the awe in her gaze. "Michael calls it the beach house. I view it as a big house that just happens to be located at the beach. Do you like it?"

"Did you expect me not to?"

"It is a little isolated."

She tried not to laugh. There seemed to be nothing but beach around for miles. "Who needs people when you've got a house like this?"

He chuckled and pointed toward the back of the house. "Come. I'll show you to your room."

He led her down a hallway. She could smell the salt in the air and her pulse leaped with excitement. She practically skipped down the hall.

For as long as she could remember, Caris had loved the ocean. As a child, the beach was the only place she'd go with her family without complaining.

Caris took a deep breath as Alex unlocked a rattan door.

"This is your room."

She stared at the windows that made up one full wall of

the bedroom. Outside, the waves crashed along the shoreline in a soothing yet arousing rhythm.

Caris hadn't seen any of the other rooms, but this had to be the best room in the house. She couldn't imagine anything better. She stepped inside. "This is all for me?"

She wasn't aware she'd spoken aloud until Alex answered her, his honey-coated voice so close to her ear a shiver ran up her spine. "You sound surprised. Why wouldn't this all be for you?"

"I'm not a guest, Alex. I'm here to work."

He folded his arms and surveyed her languidly through half-shut eyes. "Would you rather I put you in a closet somewhere at the back of the house?"

She faced the glass doors that opened directly onto the beach. "Is that where Harrison's staying?"

"Harrison has a suite in the upstairs wing. He's got everything a working lawyer could ask for—computer, air-conditioning and no view of the beach to distract him."

"It sounds perfect for Harrison."

"I tried to place you both in rooms you would enjoy and feel comfortable in," Alex said.

She bristled, wondering if she had imagined sexual discrimination. "I'm a lawyer just like Harrison. Why didn't you give me a room like his?"

"Would you rather have a room like his?" Alex asked. "All you have to do is tell me and I'll have your suitcase delivered upstairs."

She paused, then said, "No. Honestly, I'd rather stay here." She gazed at the ocean again, her body tingling with each crashing wave.

"That's what I thought."

She ducked her head, wishing he weren't so adept at reading her. She feared she'd lost her poker face, possibly for good.

If the room Harrison was staying in was perfect for a busy, successful attorney, what did it mean that she preferred this room, with its sensual ambience and soft breezes coming through the open windows?

Alex took out a large key similar to ones she saw in old movies and placed it on the bureau. She picked it up. It looked older than she did.

"It may not look like much," he said, nodding at the antique key, "but it works. The afternoon is yours to do with as you like. Dinner is at six."

She bounced the key in her hand. "Do the other rooms on this floor have direct access to the beach like this?"

"Only this room and the one next door."

"And who gets that room?"

"Does it matter?"

She stared at him, wondering why he had evaded her question. "Not really. I'm just curious."

"The other room belongs to me." His fingers played with a button on his shirt. "Does that bother you?"

It seemed a challenge, so she answered with one of her own. "Should it?"

He smiled at her, a calculated smile. "Only if you don't trust me."

"I trust you."

He cocked his head, surveying her with an intentness that made her breath catch. "I don't think so. Not yet. But you will." He turned to leave. "I'll see you at dinner."

The last thing she saw before the doors closed behind him were his brown eyes aglow with something she was afraid to describe.

After a servant who looked too young to drive brought her bag from the car, Caris showered away the dust from the trip. Clad in a fluffy white towel, she searched through her suitcase for the two bathing suits she'd asked her secretary to buy.

It had been a risk to send her secretary clothes shopping for her. Linda's style was all spandex and sequins. But there hadn't been time to ask the shopping service. The only alternative would have been to go shopping herself. Caris would rather spend a week swimming in her best business suit than step foot in any of D.C.'s crowded shops.

The first swimsuit was black, with white polka dots, a creation made for someone's grandmother. She stepped into it and eyed herself in the bedroom's full-length gilded mirror.

She'd asked Linda to choose a bathing suit appropriate for a lawyer giving a summation in court. Linda had succeeded all too well.

But just because she wanted to appear respectable didn't mean she wanted to look ugly.

Caris stripped off the suit, hoping the second suit, the one she'd had Linda buy as a backup, would be better.

The other suit turned out to be a red bikini, and Caris groaned, her cheeks burning at the thought of wearing so little material in front of another human being. On the back of the sales receipt Linda had scrawled, "Have a little fun for once! With love, Linda."

Caris grimaced. Wouldn't Linda ever understand that Caris, a female lawyer in a predominately male field, couldn't enjoy the things Linda could?

Last Christmas, Linda had been Caris's Secret Santa and her gift to Caris had been a red velvet dress with a side slit cut higher than the moral majority at the firm would have liked, and lower than most of the younger male lawyers would have liked.

Linda had included the receipt with the gift, telling Caris, "I know it's not your style, but I think it would look fantastic on you. You can return it if you like. I won't mind. Buy yourself a new briefcase or something."

Caris never returned the gift. She rationalized it was because she hated stores, but the truth was, she loved the soft, flamboyant dress.

Every once in a while, Caris would close her apartment curtains and slip into the dress. She would dance around, enjoying the feel of the dress swaying with her movements, teasing her skin with its voluptuous softness.

But most of the time, the red dress hung in the dark of her closet, right next to the filmy negligees no one ever saw.

She held the bikini up to herself. The cups were so small she wondered if they would even cover her nipples. The briefs lived up to its name.

Something compelled her to slip into the bikini, enjoying the almost forbidden feeling of the sleek material sliding against her skin.

"Not bad," she murmured, eyeing herself in the mirror. The red bikini covered more than the basics, but it was still much more provocative than what she normally wore.

She twirled in front of the mirror, feeling a smug sense of feminine pride. With a reluctant smile, she slipped out of the bikini and back into the matronly swimsuit, feeling as though she were donning armor.

Even though the suit was so concealing it flattened all her curves, she didn't feel comfortable parading around in it. As she stepped onto the patio clad in her white terry-cloth bathrobe, she wondered what Harrison's swimsuit would be like.

Knowing Harrison, he would probably wear his business suit. Even on the beach.

ALEX LEANED BACK in the beach chair, enjoying the hot sun heating his bare chest. He hoped the tropical sun would heat the chilly emptiness that had lived inside him since he'd discovered he wasn't happy in New York.

He glanced at the closed door to Caris's room, wondering if her bathing suit would be as lawyer-like as the rest of her outfits. He sensed that the ocean was one of the few places Caris Johnson felt comfortable enough to let her hair down. At least that was how he'd managed to explain that devastating kiss they'd shared at Corazon Inlet.

"Ah, there you are."

Alex turned to see Harrison striding across the beach and

stifled his grin. The man was still wearing his work clothes. His leather-soled shoes slipped in the soft sand.

Harrison pulled a handkerchief out of his pocket and mopped his sweaty forehead. "How hot is it here? A hundred? Hundred and ten?"

"It's only about ninety, but the humidity is quite high. Why don't you change and take a swim? If you don't have a swimsuit, I'm sure we can find you one."

Harrison eyed the black bikini briefs Alex wore, with a smile more befitting a man in his eighties. "I don't think one of your suits would fit me."

Alex shook his head, trying to clear his mind of the picture of Harrison squeezing his vitals into tiny bikini briefs. "I'm sure we could find something more suitable for someone of your stature."

"I really didn't come here for a vacation, Mr. Navarro..."

"But I did, Mr. Peters," Alex broke in smoothly but firmly. "There will be plenty of time for negotiations when my sister arrives. But today, I intend to relax and have some fun. I suggest you do the same."

Harrison didn't look happy about the prospect, but nodded. "Very well then, I think I'll retreat to my air-conditioned room and check in with the office."

"That might be a little difficult."

Harrison whirled so quickly he almost fell over. "Why?"

"No phones."

Harrison gaped at him. "Do you mean to tell me that a man of your wealth and stature does not possess a telephone?"

"I've got telephones," Alex said. "Just not up here."

Not anymore, anyway. He'd had them ripped out, in case his father's will got out of probate before the negotiations were completed. Once it was discovered that Navarro Investments was nearly broke, Alex's negotiating power would be nil.

"How can you not have a telephone?" Harrison asked, clearly aghast.

"Don't need one." Alex flung his arm toward the ocean. "Can you honestly tell me you'd rather phone your office than swim in the ocean?"

"Yes."

Sad thing was, Harrison was probably telling the truth.

"Sometimes it's not so bad to be out of touch," Alex said. "Some might even consider it relaxing. You should try it sometime."

"But, what if there's an emergency?"

There was always the cellular phone in the trunk of his car, but Alex wasn't about to tell Harrison about that. "It's not that far back to town. And there's a phone at Corazon Inlet, about an hour from here."

Harrison shook his head grimly. "We'll have to put in phone lines for the resort."

"Of course," Alex said, trying not to act smug. And while they were at it, they could bring the phone lines into the center of the island, a barely populated region the phone company hadn't considered profitable enough to equip, but Alex knew needed the service.

Harrison's shoes slipped in the sand and he glared at his feet, as if he could make the forces of nature obey him. "You really don't have a phone?" He sounded so upset Alex almost took pity on him. Almost.

"No phone, Harrison."

Harrison straightened his shoulders. "I'll find something to do. You can never go over a legal document too many times." He strode away, losing his battle with the slippery sand.

Alex pitied Harrison. Here they were, on one of the most beautiful and unspoiled beaches of the Gulf Coast and all Harrison could think about was work and air-conditioning.

"Hi."

Caris stood behind him, covered in an immense white

terry-cloth bathrobe. He wondered for a brief exciting moment if she was naked underneath.

"Mind if I join you?"

He stood and pulled another beach chair from the patio. "Please." He placed the chair on the soft sand, right next to his own.

Caris sat, still enveloped in her huge robe.

"Aren't you too warm?"

"Not really." But the bright sheen of perspiration on her face told him she lied.

"Why don't you go for a swim?"

She gazed at the water, her longing expression reminding him of his nephew's the last time they'd visited the biggest toy store in Houston. "No, I shouldn't. I should find Harrison and see if he has any work for me to do."

Alex sat in his chair and leaned his head back, his heels planted in the sand. "Suit yourself. But I banished Harrison from my sight until tomorrow. I told him to have a good time."

"Really?" She looked so interested it was all he could do not to laugh. "Where did he go?"

"Back to his air-conditioned room to go over some documents."

She glanced at the water. "I suppose one quick swim couldn't hurt."

He folded his arms across his chest, wondering if she wore a bikini under her robe.

Caris stood and shrugged out of her robe, looking as though she was trying hard not to notice him watching her.

On any other woman, Caris's swimsuit would have been disappointing. Black, with white polka dots, the suit was designed to conceal the flaws of a more imperfect body, not hide the perfection he suspected Caris Johnson possessed.

Still, his eyes traveled down her long legs, lingering at the soft dimples behind her knees. The woman did have marvelous legs. She'd captured her hair in the bun he normally found so unappealing, but now, he noticed, the bun allowed the soft paleness of her neck to be exposed to view. Alex longed to kiss her there, to inhale the smooth warmth at her nape.

"What?" Caris asked.

She'd caught him staring. Again. "I just realized, that is the perfect swimsuit for a lawyer to wear. You could probably wear it into a courtroom and still win your case in a professional and lawyer-like fashion."

Caris looked down at herself, a sad expression in her eyes. "I hate it, too," she whispered and turned away.

He admired her lithe strength as she ran toward the ocean and dived in. She emerged sputtering a few feet from shore.

"How is it?" He cupped his hands around his mouth, yelling so she could hear him.

"Wonderful!" She waved her hand. "Come on in!"

He didn't need to be asked twice. In a second, he dived into the water.

Alex heard her gasp when he emerged in front of her. He was near enough to touch her. He could smell the warmth of her body mixing with the cool salty tang of the ocean. He needed to touch her, needed to kiss her again. Needed to rediscover the sea nymph he'd met so briefly at Corazon Inlet.

He licked his lips, tasting the salty brine, remembering the taste of Caris.

He took a step toward her. "Caris..."

She smoothed a hand over her hair in an action he now recognized as discomfort, and stepped back. "Alex," she warned.

"Right," he said, wishing circumstances were different and just for today he could be a man ruled only by his passions and not the president of Navarro Investments, a man who was governed by logic.

He dunked his head. Warm water flowed over his scalp, doing little to soothe his raging hormones. Just once, he wished an Arctic current would flow here. Maybe then, he'd get his mind back on business and away from Caris Johnson. With a disconcerting jolt, he realized that only a silky layer of Lycra and warm ocean water separated their naked bodies.

Caris leaned her head back in the water and Alex stared at the curve of her throat, feeling like a hungry lion viewing his next meal.

"I can't believe you're willing to turn this place into a resort," Caris said.

Alex floated in place next to her, aching to touch her. "What do you mean?"

"If I owned this piece of paradise, you couldn't pay me enough to leave."

"I agree. There's more to life than money."

She turned to look at him, something akin to surprise shining in her eyes. "Then why are you selling it?"

He forced himself to think about the deal and not the drops of water he hungered to lick from her lips. "What if you knew that the people who lived here and relied on you needed so much more than you could provide for them? What if you felt responsible for them and felt it was your duty to procure the things you couldn't provide?"

She stood in the water, the ocean lapping at her breasts like a lover's caress. He crushed his hands into fists to keep from reaching for her.

"I guess I would have to decide which was more important to me. My wishes or theirs," Caris said.

"And?"

She stared at him for a moment. Her thoughts, for once, were camouflaged from his view. "I don't like to deal in hypotheticals, Alex."

"You're a lawyer. That's what you were trained to do."

She shook her head, her wet bun sliding down her neck. He wanted to release it for good.

"Doesn't mean I like it." She waded toward shore then turned to face him. "It's too easy for me to see all points of view and empathize with each of them."

"So which side do you pick?" Alex asked, not really caring about her answer, but unwilling to let her leave.

She turned away again. "Whichever side pays my salary."

"Caris, don't go."

She ran up the beach and retrieved her robe. "I have to go to work." She turned and smiled at him one last time as she shrugged into her robe and then, without another backward glance, she disappeared into the house.

Alex gave one frustrated growl then dived into the water, swimming from the shore as though his life depended on it.

7

CARIS SHIVERED, wondering why Harrison needed to air-condition his room until it felt as frigid as D.C. in winter. She crossed her legs and heard the reassuring whisper of her stockings. She felt in control now that she was clothed in a business suit and her hair was once again tamed inside a bun.

"I can't figure this guy out." Harrison paced the floor of his sitting room.

"Who?"

Harrison shot her a look that someone else would have termed rude, but Caris knew was mere impatience. She reminded herself not to take offense.

"Navarro. Keep your mind on the business at hand, Caris. Don't let the sun and sand fool you into relaxing your guard. That's just what he wants us to do, relax. And then he'll attack."

"Alex?"

Harrison sighed, a sound of pure exasperation. "Of course, Alex."

Caris sighed, wishing she had stayed in the water with Alex instead of hibernating with Harrison in his traveling law library. But it had seemed too dangerous to stay, what with him staring at her as though he wanted to ravish her in the tide. And she, wishing he would. "I'm sorry. It's just that he doesn't seem the manipulative type."

Harrison clicked his teeth in a sound that infuriated her. "Poor, sweet, naive Caris."

She burned at the condescension in his voice, but held her tongue.

"Alex Navarro is a shark. Just because he looks good in a black bikini doesn't mean he's not dangerous."

He cocked his head and Caris felt the blush she had never been able to control highlight her discomfort.

"You haven't let Navarro seduce you, have you?"

"Me? Of course not!"

She did her best to portray outward indignation, but on the inside she was a mass of nerves and insecurity. Was she being seduced by Alex? Had she underestimated him, assumed he would play fairly and aboveboard simply because she liked him?

Had she let down her guard?

If so, that was about to change.

She lifted her chin in resolution. "You can count on me, Harrison." She sat up in her chair, as though by straightening her spine she could strengthen her resolve.

Harrison smiled. "That's a good girl."

She wanted to hit him for that remark but instead she opened her laptop computer. "What's our next move?"

Harrison tapped a finger against his chin. "Tell me what you know about Michael Navarro."

Michael was one of Alex's weaknesses. Caris opened her mouth to tell Harrison that, but then closed it. For some reason, she felt as though she'd be betraying Alex if she told Harrison. She rubbed one fingertip over her computer case, then scrolled through the background report she'd compiled before she left D.C., seeking something less damaging to reveal.

"Michael's a good student. As a matter of fact, he's the second-best student Harvard has ever had in their MBA program."

"Alex being the first, of course." Harrison rolled his eyes. "Tell me something I don't know, Caris. What's Michael doing here? I thought you said he'd be in the middle of finals now and we'd only be dealing with Alex."

All of her research showed Michael took his studies very seriously. So what was he doing here?

"I don't know," Caris said finally.

"Well, maybe you should find out."

She felt chastised and her skin burned. She lowered her gaze to her computer screen and typed "Find out about Michael," not because she was in any danger of forgetting Harrison's request, but because she couldn't bear to look at the man's accusing gaze any longer.

"And the sister. Kate," Harrison said. "What's her story?"

"I think she left her husband."

"No one leaves Paul Miller, the richest man in Texas."

Kate hadn't left Paul Miller, the richest man in Texas. She'd left Paul Miller, the biggest jerk in Texas. But Caris held her tongue, sensing Harrison wouldn't understand.

"Why would Kate divorce Paul Miller?" Harrison asked.

Because he's an SOB, Caris thought, but aloud she said, "Maybe she doesn't love him anymore."

"Love?" Harrison snorted. "Since when does love have anything to do with money?"

Caris had no answer for that, and it surprised her. A week ago, she would have agreed wholeheartedly with Harrison. She'd always believed a person could put up with almost anything if the price was right. Now she wasn't so sure.

"It doesn't matter, really," Harrison said. "I doubt Kate will be much of an influence on this deal."

Caris fought the urge to defend Kate, even though she sensed Harrison's assessment was correct. "Kate will vote with Alex," Caris said. "I'm not sure how Michael will vote."

Harrison narrowed his eyes. "You're not sure? You'd better be sure. That's the only reason I brought you, Caris."

Caris resisted the urge to remind him he'd only brought her because Martin Joffrey had insisted. "Don't worry, Harrison. I'll be sure."

He eyed her for a moment longer, his gray-eyed gaze chillier than his air-conditioned room. "Don't make me regret putting my faith in you."

Caris bit her lip. Harrison hadn't put any faith in her. And if she didn't stop thinking about Alex and cigarettes, no one else at the firm would, either.

"You can count on me, Harrison."

"Good." He turned to pace. "Let's go over the offer again, shall we?"

For the next few hours they discussed strategies and reviewed research already compiled on Alex and Navarro Investments. By the time a blushing and stammering teenage maid informed them dinner would be ready in ten minutes, Caris's fingers and back ached from typing. Her eyes burned with a mixture of exhaustion and overuse.

Harrison closed his law book and stood. "Good. We're ready for whatever Navarro throws at us."

Caris stood and stretched. "I'm going to freshen up. I'll meet you at dinner."

At first the warmer temperature of the hallway felt good, warming bones that had been chilled for too long. Then she began to sweat, her jacket sticking to her back.

"I missed you this afternoon."

She whirled, surprised to see Alex standing behind her. He wore a red T-shirt. The bottom edge of his swimsuit was tantalizingly sweet to her eyes. He shifted, showing more of the shiny Lycra, and she followed the trail of hair up his muscular thighs until it disappeared beneath the black cloth.

She raised her gaze to the relative safety of his face. His smile told her he knew exactly what she'd been looking at. And that he liked it.

She tossed her head, willing herself not to blush. "I was working."

"You know what they say, Caris. All work and no play—"

"Gets Jill a corporate partnership," she interrupted, trying to keep her temper under control. "I'm well aware of the saying, Mr. Navarro."

He cocked his head. "So we're back to formalities, are we?"

"We were always formal, Alex." She disappeared into the bedroom.

"Not always, Caris." He stood in the doorway, trying not to feel disappointed. It had taken only four hours of being with Harrison Peters for Caris Johnson to revert to the prickly, nervous lawyer he'd picked up at the airport yesterday. What a shame. He so much preferred her smiling and flinging witty banter at him as the gulf breezes teased the hair from its bun.

He termed it flirting, but he knew that Caris would describe it as friendly conversation between business associates.

What would it take for her to admit there was more than mere business building between them?

His stomach constricted as he realized that somewhere along the way he had stopped thinking of a relationship with Caris in terms of something that must never happen into something that *had* to happen.

ALEX STARED OUT at the ocean, the emptiness inside him returning, almost as all-encompassing as the darkness around him.

Some might say this feeling had overtaken him after his father's death and his return to the island, but Alex knew that it had always been with him. Since college, he'd spent an enormous amount of time and energy trying to fill that bleak void with work and friends, and with women who were always gone by morning.

Now, on the island he'd always considered home, Alex found the darkness wouldn't go away.

He was exhausted. He thought it would be easy maintaining the facade of a financially prosperous family business fo the week it would take to clinch this deal. He hadn't counted on Michael's unexpected arrival complicating his plans. Or Kate leaving her husband and throwing John's composure into a frenzy.

John had promised he'd take on most of the responsibilities for the inexperienced house staff, leaving Alex free to concentrate on the business deal. But then Kate had shown up—fragile, confused and lovely—and John was practically worthless.

Alex would have been amused at Kate and John's attempts to pretend to be unconcerned by each other, but he was worried this deal was going to fall through. More than that, he was envious that they had finally gotten their second chance at love. He had to face the truth. There was something missing from his life. More correctly, there was *someone* missing from his life.

Kate had Thomas and memories of a marriage that had worked at least in the beginning. And now, if the lovestruck gazes in both hers and John's eyes were anything to be believed, she had John. Michael had his casual affairs, each more tempestuous and vapid than the last. What did Alex have?

Nothing. Nothing but responsibility for a fading empire and a poverty-stricken island. And a fear that he would always be alone.

He walked farther into the night. Although he could barely see the lights of the house, he could still hear the pounding beat of the rock band Michael had impetuously invited to play for the evening. Michael's friends had descended on the house like a swarm of army ants on a jar of honey. Their drunken laughter gave him chills even in this heat. Despite his loneliness, he couldn't bear to return to the house. A house that rightly belonged to him but no longer felt like his home. Not since Michael's friends had descended from the mainland and turned his peaceful weekend retreat into a raucous dance hall.

He walked faster.

Thoughts of Caris looking pale and worried over dinner teased him. She'd barely eaten anything, then retreated to her room, claiming a headache.

He'd thought of checking on her but then Michael's friends had arrived, taking over the house, and Alex had felt the urge to flee.

As he left, a woman he had never met before attached herself to his arm and Alex knew that all he had to do was nod his head and she'd spend the night in his bed. But she wasn't the woman he wanted in his bed.

Alex used to enjoy women like that. In New York, he'd played the game and taken whatever these women offered; a few hours in bed, a few moments of pleasure.

His relationships, if they could even be called that, never lasted long. Work had always taken up most of his time. Now that he'd left his eighteen-hour-a-day job, he found he had the time, but he didn't have the heart.

Alex stared at the ocean, the sounds of the party now as soft and inconsequential as the buzzing of a mosquito. He let the music of the ocean roll over him, filling the empty spaces inside him, and wondered when the best time of his life was supposed to start.

CARIS HURRIED AWAY from the house. She felt more ashamed of herself at this moment than she had ever felt in her entire life. Even more ashamed than that day in the third grade when the principal had caught her and Johnny Renquist kissing and used their example at the school assembly as proof of morality gone astray.

Today, she had topped all of the less than pure things she had done in her life. Today she had done something she normally prosecuted other people for.

Today, she had become a thief.

Caris stared at the pack of cigarettes clenched in her hand.

It seemed like a gift from God. Cigarettes, *her* brand of cigarettes, lying forgotten on a table in the main hallway.

She'd been looking for aspirin, but when she saw the pack, she hadn't been able to resist.

She'd only planned to take one cigarette to see if her brand would provide the pleasure she craved without any side effects, but here she was, holding the entire pack and hiding out on the beach like a fugitive. She almost felt too guilty to enjoy the cigarette she risked her career for. Almost.

Caris stopped walking. The beach was empty. She could smoke in peace.

She slipped one cigarette out of the pack, her fingers trembling.

"Just out for a stroll?"

Caris jumped and dropped the cigarette on the ground.

"Here, let me."

Alex bent down to retrieve the cigarette from the sand. He brushed it off, then held it out to her. "Now I know your secret."

"Secret?"

His eyes were shadowed so she couldn't tell if his smile was genuine or merely for show, like that of a lawyer playacting in court.

"You smoke." He still held out the cigarette.

She backed away from him, the pack of cigarettes hidden behind her back.

"You dropped it," he said. "I saw you drop it. Here."

She felt like a fool. All evidence linked her to the cigarette, but she dropped the pack on the sand behind her and continued to play innocent. "I don't know what you're talking about."

He cocked his head, still holding out the cigarette to her. "Why won't you just admit it? There's no crime in smoking. At least not yet."

"All right, all right. I admit it!" She grabbed the cigarette and flung it to the sand. "There. Are you happy now? You know my dirty little secret. I smoke! I'm a chain-smoker and I haven't had a cigarette in two days, ever since I got on that awful plane with Harrison Peters!"

He had the audacity to laugh.

"Don't you dare laugh at me!"

Tears pooled in her eyes and she whirled away, unwilling to let him see how close she was to the edge.

"Hey, Caris, I'm sorry." He stroked her arm lightly. "If I'd known you were feeling so bad, I wouldn't have teased you. I'm sorry."

She wiped her eyes and tossed her head, trying to regain the composure she feared she'd left locked in one of her office drawers in D.C.

"Since you've lasted this long without a cigarette, why don't you try for a little longer? I've heard it only takes four days to remove all nicotine from your system."

"Four days of hell!" She whirled around. "You have no idea what I'm going through!"

"You're right. I don't have any idea what you're going through." His voice was still light but she could sense the anger lurking as a rough undercoat. "But then, I didn't get myself addicted to a cancer-causing, life-threatening habit."

"You think you know everything, don't you?" she muttered.

He picked up the package of cigarettes she thought he hadn't seen and tossed them to her. "Here. Knock yourself out. Smoke the entire pack. If you run out, I'll even take you into town to get some more."

He walked away and she realized she had overreacted, yet again.

"Alex, wait."

He stood still, waiting.

"I'm sorry. I shouldn't have said that. You're right. I did this to myself and I have no one to blame but me."

He turned around, but she couldn't look at him. It was so

much easier to stare at the cigarettes in her hand than see the disappointment she knew must show in his face.

"You may not believe this, but I'm not normally like this." She laughed nervously. "As a matter of fact, most people think I'm cool as a block of ice." She winced remembering her nickname. *Ice Queen.*

"They obviously don't know you very well. The moment I met you, I could see you were highly emotional."

She frowned, not enjoying the picture he painted of her. "When you saw me," she said, "I had just endured a horrific airplane landing and I was in the sixth hour of my new life without cigarettes."

"*New* life?" he asked. "Does that mean you're quitting for good?"

She stared at the cigarettes. What had once seemed like a godsend now just looked like an unhealthful addiction.

"I didn't say that," she said.

"Have you ever thought about quitting?"

She shrugged. "Sure. A few times. Usually during my annual checkup when my doctor berates me for not taking better care of myself. I also vow to join a gym and cut down on red meat," she added, before he got any ideas. "I have yet to do any of those things."

"Why don't you try it now?"

"It's too hard…"

"Have you thought about what will happen to you in the next few years?"

She frowned, confused by his change of topic. "You mean, like a plan for my life? Sure, I've got one of those."

"I'm not talking about your career path," Alex said. "I'm talking about your life."

"What do you mean?"

"Do you want to have children?"

Her insides constricted at the sweet thought of her own child; a dream that, like the lingerie and slinky red dress hidden in her closet, she shared with no one. "Possibly."

"Do you plan to smoke through your pregnancy?"

"Of course not! Don't you know how dangerous it is to smoke while you're pregnant?"

"Yes, I do. But do you? What about after your children are born? Will you smoke around them?"

She hadn't thought about that. "No."

"Tell me this, Caris. If you're willing to protect the people you care about from your smoking, why aren't you willing to protect yourself?"

She didn't know how to answer him.

He put his hands in his pants pockets and stared at her for a moment. "I'll make a deal with you."

She was instantly suspicious. "What kind of deal?"

He smiled. "You're not very trusting, are you, Caris?"

She didn't want to answer that. "What kind of a deal?" she repeated.

"If you can stay away from cigarettes for the next four days, I'll pay you a thousand dollars."

His tongue seemed to trip on the dollar amount and she watched as he fidgeted, digging his toe into the sand. He reminded her of a cardsharp who'd impulsively bet more than he could afford to lose. But why would Alex Navarro be worried about a measly thousand-dollar bet? He was rich.

"What makes you think I'll quit smoking just because you want me to?" Caris asked.

"Why did you quit smoking on the flight down?"

"My career—"

"Harrison," he interrupted. "Harrison and, in an indirect way, your career."

She narrowed her eyes. "What do you get if I don't quit smoking?"

"You."

"Excuse me?" She nearly choked on a salty breeze.

He grinned, and she knew he'd intended his comment to be construed that way. "You, working with the Job Corps volunteers, building houses and helping to repair structures on the island, for two weeks during your vacation."

"I never take a vacation."

"Then you'd better not lose."

She considered the idea for a moment. She didn't need the money, but she could always use more power during their negotiations. "A thousand dollars doesn't seem equal to what I'd be giving up."

"Name your price."

"One extra concession for the land deal."

He looked disappointed. "No. This is personal, Caris. Not business."

"Then we don't have a deal."

She turned to walk away, knowing if he stopped her before she got ten feet away, she would win. If not, the deal was off.

Five feet, six feet, seven, eight.

Ten.

At the eleven-foot marker, she whirled around. "You were going to let me walk away, weren't you?"

He grinned. "I would have followed you. After all—" he nodded toward the lights of the house "—I know where you live."

She walked toward him, not ready to give up. "One extra concession during the deal, but you get to pick which one."

"No concessions. A thousand dollars, and if I lose, I'll spend two weeks doing volunteer work for any charity you pick."

That threw her. Why would Alex Navarro bet two weeks of his life instead of more money? Surely his time was more valuable than that.

"Two thousand," she said, not caring about the money, just wondering how far she could push him.

He held out his hand. "One thousand, two weeks working for your favorite charity and I'll throw in a guided snorkeling tour of the sunken Spanish galleons around Navarro Island."

She wavered, knowing she would lose. But she could still have the last word. "You have to buy me lunch after the tour."

He took her hand, chuckling. "Deal."

She shook his hand. How could it be so warm despite the chilly winds coming off the ocean?

She stared at the cigarettes in her other hand. "I think I just quit smoking."

"I think you did."

She continued to stare at the familiar logo on the packet.

"Would it help if I got rid of them for you? You know, out of sight, out of mind."

"No. It helps knowing that if I really lose my mind, I can have a cigarette."

"You can always have a cigarette, Caris. You have the power to say yes or no to them."

She nodded and held the cigarettes out to him. "Unless, of course, you'd rather hold them because of our wager?"

"I trust you, Caris. Besides, the only person you'll be cheating is yourself."

She nodded toward the house. "I guess I'll go back in. The sooner I get to sleep, the quicker these four days will go."

"Sleep well."

Her gaze dropped, imagining Alex sleeping, naked. And her curled around his hard, hot skin. And then neither of them were sleeping at all. She looked up to find him still watching her. She shook her head to clear it of the warm, sensual haze. "I don't get it. Why does it matter to you whether I quit smoking or not?"

"Because I care about you, Caris."

She opened her mouth, then shut it again, not at all sure what she had planned to say.

"Sleep well."

He turned away and walked along the shoreline, away

from the noise and lights of the house. She watched him until he disappeared into the shadows of the night.

SHE COULDN'T SLEEP.

Caris glanced at the clock and saw it was only three minutes later than the last time she'd checked—4:07. If she didn't get some sleep soon, she'd be useless in the morning.

She patted her covers, wishing she wasn't alone. Wishing she had someone to talk to. Wishing she had someone here to distract her and have her thinking about something besides cigarettes.

Someone whose fingers would warm a path along the stiff muscles of her neck, easing the stress, easing her tension. His hand would tighten deliciously, and he would pull her toward him. Her lips would part and his breath would warm her soul.

Then they would…

Caris shook her head. If she started thinking like that, she'd never get to sleep!

Her hands shook as she rearranged the covers, resisting the urge to throw them off and run screaming into the ocean. The music from Michael's party almost drowned out the soft roar of the surf. Her nerves were stretched tighter than the strings of the electric guitar she could hear whining in the distance and she wanted to howl in harmony with it.

She was going crazy. She needed a cigarette. She needed…
Alex.

She heard him walking down the hall, his step as familiar to her as her own heartbeat. His footsteps didn't slow as he reached his bedroom door; instead, he headed straight for her room. She held her breath.

There was a soft knock on her door and she was out of bed, tugging her T-shirt over her hips before she'd even decided she was going to let him in.

She opened the door. Alex stood in the doorway, his gaze

warm, his smile wicked. "Somehow I knew you'd be awake. You look tense."

"I am tense."

His smile deepened. "I have just the thing to help."

Her heart hopped excitedly, a little warmth settling in her belly, and lower. "Help?"

He grinned. "With quitting smoking, of course."

Her heart sank and she could barely summon a smile when he handed her a small box wrapped in red tissue paper. "What's this?"

"I suspect it's not what either of us really needs, but..." His shrug spoke of regret. He picked up her hand and kissed her knuckles so swiftly she barely had time to feel it. "Mmm." He allowed her to pull her hand back, then winked. "Salty."

She could only stare at him, wishing she had the nerve to pull him into her room and lock the door behind them, keeping the rest of the world away until they were both able to sleep.

"Open it after I'm gone."

She watched him walk next door and waited until he'd gone into the adjoining bedroom before shakily closing her bedroom door.

She sat on the bed, bubbling with nervous anticipation, and ripped into the box. Packages of gum—everything from adult-style sugar-free spearmint to sugary bubble gum guaranteed to make one's teeth rot—spilled onto the bed.

She was still smiling when she turned out the light and tried to fall asleep.

8

CARIS HEADED toward the main staircase, wondering if a headache could be fatal. When she'd woken this morning, a huge wad of chewing gum wedged in the corner of her mouth, she'd had to lie there for a few moments, waiting for the pain in her head to subside.

Alex had said it would only take four days to remove all nicotine traces from her body. But Caris was afraid that when the nicotine was killed off, she'd be dead, too.

"Good morning!"

Caris winced as Harrison's voice bounced off the inside of her skull like the silver ball in a game of pinball.

"You look ill, Caris," Harrison said as he caught up to her, surprising her with his concern. "Perhaps you should skip today's tour of the beachfront property."

"Thank you, Harrison, but I'm sure I'll be fine after breakfast."

"I don't want to catch whatever you have." Harrison stepped away, shattering the illusion of care, then turned toward the dining room.

"Thanks for your concern," Caris muttered under her breath. She followed him into the dining room.

"Good morning, Caris," Alex said. "I trust you had a pleasant sleep." His hair was still wet from his recent shower and he smelled deliciously like shampoo and potent male.

Caris smiled weakly, her head pounding a fierce request for nicotine. "Thank you, I did," she lied, sinking into a chair.

"I'd like to begin discussing the contract," Harrison said.

"In due time." Alex reached for the coffee carafe on the table. "Coffee, Caris?"

She held out her cup. "Thank you."

"I don't see why we need to wait, Alex," Harrison said, the familiar whine coloring his voice. "What are you waiting for? A better offer?"

Caris held her breath as Alex poured, her shaky hand creating slight ripples in her coffee.

Alex put down the carafe in a controlled movement. "We are waiting for my sister, Kate, the third owner of Navarro Investments. But she's resting." He picked up his coffee cup. "She had a rough night."

Alex's hand trembled and Caris suddenly noticed the dark shadows beneath his eyes. She suspected he hadn't been walking on the beach those hours before he came to her room, but had spent most of the night helping Kate cope with whatever crisis she was experiencing.

Harrison sighed. "There's nothing that says we can't begin negotiations—"

"*I say*," Alex said, his tone cool yet firm.

As Caris watched the interaction between Harrison and Alex, a smooth shiver of excitement licked a path through her body.

"But—"

"*Enough.*"

Although Alex never raised his voice, the warning in his tone was unmistakable. If Harrison continued to push, this deal was as good as dead. She waited, watching Harrison, hoping Martin Joffrey had been wrong and Harrison did have some professional instincts.

Harrison dipped his head. "As you wish."

Caris let out a shaky breath.

"Croissant?"

Alex looked barely flustered, holding out a tray of flaky pastry. Caris shook her head. The way she felt now, she'd be lucky to keep her coffee down.

"Morning, all!" Michael burst into the room.

Caris downed two more aspirin with her coffee, wishing it were possible to live in a silent movie.

Michael sat at the table and motioned to John, who was standing in the corner. "Get me some eggs, bacon and a fresh pot of coffee. And be quick about it."

John cocked one eyebrow and looked as if he was about to say something vulgar, but Alex spoke first.

"Mind your manners, Michael."

"It's his job, isn't it?" Michael asked. "Or is there something you'd like to tell me about this unorthodox working relationship?"

Alex opened his mouth to reply, but John interrupted. "How would you like your eggs, Michael?"

"Over easy."

"With pleasure." With a bow that looked more mocking than respectful, John left. Caris could tell from the smug expression on Michael's face that he hadn't even noticed John's less than polite retreat.

"I'm surprised to see you up so bright and early after last night's party, Michael," Alex said.

Michael turned to Alex and shot his brother a look Caris couldn't even classify as polite. "I couldn't afford to miss today's tour, now, could I?"

Alex frowned. "I don't know what you mean, Michael, but you're welcome to join us today."

Michael bared his teeth in what might pass for a smile. "With an invitation like that, how could I possibly not join you?" He turned to Caris. "You're looking pale, Caris. Didn't you sleep well?"

"I've told her to stay here and rest," Harrison said, "but as is typical of these females, she's acting stubborn."

Caris burned. The only way this could get worse was if one of the men asked if she was experiencing menstrual cramps.

"I'll be fine," she said in a clipped tone. She held out her coffee cup as a young housemaid brought the pot to her.

"Caris looks just great to me," Alex said, "although slightly overdressed for our trip today. You might want to change into something more comfortable, Caris."

Caris looked down at her business suit, one of her most comfortable linen outfits. "What's wrong with this?"

"Nothing's wrong," Alex said. "It's just that here on the coast, the heat and humidity can be almost unbearable. In addition, we'll be walking in deep sand."

She clenched her hands under the table. Why wasn't he criticizing Harrison's clothing? "I believe I'm dressed appropriately, thank you."

"For a law office, yes, but not for—"

"I'm fine."

He gazed at her for another moment, then turned to Harrison. "Harrison, I'd advise you of the same thing."

Harrison chuckled. "No offense, Alex, but I don't think khaki pants and cotton shirts are my style." He nodded disparagingly at Alex's outfit.

"Just a suggestion, no offense was meant."

John walked back into the room holding a plate of bacon and eggs, which he placed with a flourish before Michael. "Here you are, sir. I cooked them myself and gave them my own personal attention."

Caris was reminded of her first college roommate, Alice, who had worked her way through school as a waitress in one of Connecticut's most exclusive restaurants. Caris remembered Alice gleefully telling her of spitting on one boorish customer's food, then serving it to him, her polite smile never faltering.

"Enjoy." John's broad smile looked just like Alice's.

Michael stared at the plate of eggs, then at John. Grimacing, he pushed the plate away. "All of a sudden, I'm not very hungry."

John picked up the plate, murmuring, "Pity."

Alex pulled his chair from the table. "I guess we're ready to go, then."

Caris nodded, picturing a beach town she'd once seen in a travel brochure.

Pictures in travel brochures had never even hinted at the blast of heat that overpowered Caris as soon as she stepped out of the air-conditioned house. It was so humid she felt as though she were swimming. As she took a breath of thick, soupy air, she wished she'd changed clothes as Alex had suggested.

Her linen suit, so comfortable in the air-conditioned house, was heavy with moisture. Her panty hose stuck to her legs at every step. She felt like one of the turkeys her mother used to cook every Thanksgiving in an aluminum-foil tent.

"Feeling all right?" Alex asked, moving next to her. "There's still time to change clothes. We can wait for you."

Caris did want to change into something cooler, but if a senior partner could bear the heat, so could she. She squared her shoulders. "I'm fine."

"I wish you didn't feel the need to constantly prove yourself, Caris. You can be just as good a lawyer in shorts as in a business suit."

She gave him a look that fellow lawyers had told her could freeze steam. "I don't wish to discuss my attire with you, Mr. Navarro."

With a small sigh, he pointed toward the Land Cruiser. "After you."

"I noticed quite a few ramshackle houses on the road to the beach," Harrison said, walking toward the car.

"About forty families live between town and the beach," Alex explained.

"I'd expect them to clear out by the time the merger is signed."

"No one is leaving," Alex said.

"Of course they are," Harrison said. "We'll put up a few apartment houses closer to town and move them in there.

Give them a dishwasher and a laundry room and they'll be happy."

Caris watched as Alex stood still, tightening his jaw into a formidable line. "These are people, Harrison, not merchandise to be moved. Many of these families have lived here for generations."

"So? Tell them we'll throw in a free TV or two and they'll happily move."

Alex turned from tan to red, almost as though a slow flame had been lit inside him and he were roasting from the inside out.

"I'm afraid you've misunderstood me, Harrison," Alex said, his calm voice at odds with the fire burning in his dark eyes. "The residents of Navarro Island are the reason I'm creating this resort. I want them to prosper from this deal. I'm not doing this just so some rich tourists can banish entire families from their own homes." He turned away, as though he didn't trust himself to stand so closely to Harrison without harming him.

"Now look here, Navarro—"

"No, you look here, Harrison." Alex whirled, one finger pointed like a pistol at Harrison's chest. "I thought I made it perfectly clear in my original proposal that the only way I'd ever consider taking on a partner and creating a resort was if the residents of the island were to prosper."

Harrison looked startled and Caris wondered if Martin Joffrey had conveniently forgotten to show the proposal to him, also.

"We can quite easily take our money elsewhere," Harrison said in a move Caris knew was supposed to be a threat.

All her research had shown that Alex Navarro never responded well to threats.

"I'll drive you to the airport myself." Alex gestured toward the car. "Shall we go?"

Caris saw Michael grin and understood why Joffrey had picked her for this job.

"I suggest you two gentlemen take a deep breath and a quick step back," she said. "It's not just the weather that's hot here."

They stared at her, Harrison with a mixture of annoyance and leftover rage; Alex with an emotion she didn't dare try to analyze.

"We all know why we're here," she said before either could interrupt her. "We were all willing to work together before. I see no reason why we can't continue."

Harrison sniffed haughtily. "We haven't even begun our work, bound as we are by a nonexistent timetable."

Harrison was acting like a spoiled child, and she was tempted to tell him so.

"The way I look at it, Harrison, I have something you want." Alex stepped closer until he and Harrison were almost touching. "That means we play by my rules."

"Rules are made to be broken, Navarro."

"Not my rules."

Any minute now, Caris expected to see fists. She stepped between them, feeling Alex's breath on her and shivering.

"Why don't we all take a moment to calm down before we do something we'll regret."

They stared at her again. Harrison glanced at his toes, then backed away. Alex remained where he was. The side of her arm skimmed his lean abdomen. The heat of his body soothed her.

When Alex stepped back, she realized she was shaking.

And it had nothing to do with Alex and Harrison's confrontation.

"Why don't we go see this beach?" Caris suggested.

Alex smiled at Caris, his smile warmer than the sun. "Seems as if you've saved the day once more, Caris."

Out of the corner of her eye, she saw Harrison's face tighten, and images of her future partnership floated away like a wisp of cigarette smoke. "Merely doing my job." She backed away from the two men, and away from Harrison's annoyed gaze.

"More than your job, it seems to me," Alex said, following her. He nodded at Harrison. "If your law firm doesn't do right by you, I will."

Caris remained silent. *Was that a business proposition, or something else?*

"Anyone would be happy to work with a lawyer of your caliber. And I'd be happy to vouch for you." Alex's small grin implied he knew exactly where her mind had wandered.

Caris blushed, her head spinning from the direction this argument had taken. "Thank you, but I enjoy both my work and my life in Washington."

"Winters in D.C. can be cold and dark. Haven't you ever considered moving south? Perhaps Texas?"

Harrison's face was darker than the proverbial storm cloud.

"Thank you again, Mr. Navarro, but I'm very happy at Harrison, Harrison, Joffrey and Peters."

Alex shrugged. As soon as Harrison turned away, he leaned closer and whispered, "Too bad, Caris." His voice caressed her as potently as his lips had. "We would have been great together."

He wasn't talking about a business partnership.

She should be offended. If another business acquaintance had spoken to her so familiarly, she would have been. But there was something about the way her name rolled off Alex's tongue that didn't offend Caris, but rather soothed and excited her.

Harrison claimed the front seat of the car, an honor she was willing to give up, and Caris took her seat in the back, next to Michael, who sat a little too close for Caris's comfort.

Alex started the car and turned on the air conditioner full blast. She leaned closer to the door, devouring the cool air.

"Don't worry, I won't bite," Michael said with a small laugh.

Reluctantly, she moved away from the stream of cool air, closer to Michael. "I never thought you'd bite." She smiled at him, wishing she could like Michael as much as she liked Kate and Alex. But in Michael she sensed a selfishness and an ambition that was impossible to admire. She had the impression that, unlike herself or Alex, Michael could truly harm someone if it would help his cause. Whatever his cause might be.

Michael drew a lazy circle on the back of her hand with his finger. When he leaned closer, she had to fight not to back away. "Of course, if you like being bitten, that could be arranged."

Barely concealing her revulsion, Caris tried to formulate a comment that would discourage Michael without alienating him.

"Enough!" Alex warned.

Caris could see Alex's eyes, furious and dark as he watched them in the rearview mirror.

Michael narrowed his eyes, leaned back in the seat and folded his arms.

"Are you all right, Caris?" Alex asked.

"I'm perfectly fine. And I could have handled it myself." Caris realized belatedly that she shouldn't confront Alex before negotiations had begun, but she was too angry, edgy and uncomfortable to stop her impulsive words. Luckily, Alex didn't seem to take offense.

"You shouldn't have to handle anything where my brother is concerned," Alex said.

Caris stared out the window, ignoring both Navarro men, and Alex sighed.

He'd blown it. Caris could have easily handled Michael's flirting, but the sight of his worthless younger brother putting the moves on Caris Johnson had enraged him. Uncharacteristically, he had thrown aside caution and responded impulsively.

Michael flirts with every woman he meets, a voice inside reminded Alex. *Why should it matter if he flirts with Caris?*

Alex tightened his jaw, feeling an ache he couldn't describe.

Because Caris Johnson is mine.

Alex turned off the main road and headed toward the beach. This side road hadn't been used in years. The Land Cruiser fought its way through ruts and wild growth, jostling the passengers unmercifully.

"Sorry about this." Alex gripped the wheel, trying to keep control of the bouncing vehicle. "We're almost there."

They hit a huge bump and Alex heard Harrison's teeth clatter.

"Ouch!"

He glanced in the rearview mirror. Caris was holding on to her seat for dear life, her eyes scrunched closed.

"Are you all right, Caris?"

"No! I hit my head against the top of the car."

He hit another bump, and Caris bounced, barely missing the ceiling.

"Almost there." He drove onto the sand and pulled as close to the shoreline as he dared. "We're here."

The car was strangely silent.

"Obviously," Harrison said, his teeth clenched, "that road will have to be paved."

"Obviously," Alex agreed, trying not to smile. There was an easier way to get to the beach, but Alex had chosen this route knowing that paved roads would be one less concession he'd need to barter for.

Caris fumbled with the car door and practically dived out of the car. He stepped out to help her. "Are you all right?" he asked again.

She took a shaky breath. "Just a little—" she swallowed thickly "—nauseated."

Alex felt like a heel. "We'll take the other road back. It's not as bumpy."

Caris nodded, her insides churning like the ocean at high tide. "It sure is hot," she said, trying to take her mind off her nausea. And the unsettling feel of him standing so close to her.

"I warned you to take off those clothes," he said in a teasing voice.

He was right, but she would never tell him that. "I'll be fine." Her clothing was strangling her, sweat gland by sweat gland, and she longed to rip her panty hose into shreds.

She felt his concerned gaze on her and repeated, "I'm fine. Really."

She closed the car door with more panache than she knew she possessed. "Ready whenever you are."

Harrison stepped from the front seat, fanning himself with his linen handkerchief. "Don't these people believe in air-conditioning?"

Alex stared at him for a moment. "How do you propose to air-condition the great outdoors, Harrison?"

"Believe me, if I lived here, I'd find a way." Harrison turned slowly, checking the empty beach. "So this is the property you're asking so much money for."

Caris groaned. *Subtle, Harrison. Really subtle.*

"This is it."

Caris brushed at the damp hair clinging to her nape. For the first time in days, she didn't long for a cigarette. Instead, she wanted a tall glass of iced tea. Preferably big enough for her to bathe in.

She felt like hell. Between the heat, too much coffee on an empty stomach and nicotine withdrawal, every part of her ached or burned or churned. Reminding herself that she'd never make partner if she got sick, Caris tried to swallow the nausea undulating inside her.

She winced as a load of hot sand slithered inside one of her shoes, burning her.

"It'll be easier if we walk closer to the ocean. The sand is packed more densely there." Alex walked toward the shore and Caris followed quickly, trying not to fall. The sand shifted each time she took a step, and her heels kept sinking, showering her feet with what felt like miniature burning coals. It was small consolation to see Harrison having almost as much trouble in his leather loafers. Alex and Michael, both in bare feet protected by sandals, appeared fleet-footed and sure of themselves in the shifting sand.

When they reached the tide line, Alex stepped into the water, soaking his feet as well as the bottom of his trousers. He grinned at Caris. "Try it. I guarantee it will be more comfortable than walking in heels."

It was an appealing idea, but she couldn't imagine Harrison voting to hire a partner who he'd seen on a beach, taking off her panty hose. "I'm fine," she lied as her heels sank farther into the sand.

Alex motioned toward his left. "This is the beginning of the beach property. It goes down another eight miles to the southern tip of the island, then curves back around." He walked farther down and Caris followed, establishing a strange rhythm in her sinking heels.

Walk, sink, pull. Walk, sink, pull. It was exhausting. She glanced back, watching as the ocean erased the square holes her shoes had made.

While they walked, Harrison and Alex finally engaged in a sensible discussion regarding the improvements that could be made to the empty beach. Caris tried to keep up. But the farther she walked, the more overheated and queasy she became. Eventually she was struggling to merely remain upright.

The early-morning sun burned her scalp. She pulled off her suit jacket. Still sweating, Caris tugged at the top button of her blouse, then at the second. She wanted to unbutton even more, but figured Harrison wouldn't look kindly upon her showing off her brassiere.

Caris squinted ahead. There were two lone sunbathers at the end of the beach. They appeared too close together to be doing anything but...

She stopped. "I think we've gone far enough."

Harrison turned to her, surprised. "No matter what your thoughts, Caris, we do need to view the entire beach."

Alex looked questioningly at her and Caris nodded toward the couple who were so engrossed in each other.

"Oh," Alex said. He grinned. "One of the benefits of a secluded beach." He pointed toward the tree line. "Why don't we head over there and leave those two some privacy."

Harrison turned red as he obviously realized what the couple on the beach were doing. "Well, I never..."

And Harrison probably hadn't.

Caris would have giggled if she hadn't felt so ill. The tree-lined area looked cooler, but so far away. As she walked, the sand burned her feet and stuck to her already sweating legs. She closed her eyes and turned toward the ocean, drinking in the cooling breezes, trying to gather strength for the long walk.

"Caris?"

Caris nodded but didn't open her eyes. She could smell the lovers' suntan lotion and hear the groans and moans they made pleasuring each other. "I just need some air." She took a deep breath but couldn't seem to get any oxygen into her lungs.

"You're outside," Harrison sputtered. "How much air can you possibly need?"

Alex placed a hand on her elbow. "Why don't we go back to the house. We can come back later, perhaps when it's cooler."

Caris shivered, overcome with everything. The scent of coconut oil and sex filled her nostrils, and her body burned with heat and tension. She would kill for a cigarette, but what she really wanted was to rip off her clothes and dive into the ocean.

And when she had cooled off, she wanted to emerge from the sea, still naked, and find Alex waiting for her. Naked, hard and ready for her like no other man had ever been ready for her before.

"Caris?" Alex asked.

She heard a moan; it tantalized her with all the sensations she'd traded for an air-conditioned law office.

"What do you need, Caris?" Alex asked.

A life, she wanted to say. But when she opened her mouth to speak, her ears began to buzz and the world faded away.

CARIS WOKE with a start.

"It's all right. You're safe."

She stared at Alex, wondering what he was doing there. And why it seemed so natural for him to be sitting on the side of her bed. "What happened?"

"You fainted. How are you feeling?"

"Fainted?" She couldn't believe it. "I never faint. You must be mistaken."

Alex chuckled. "Believe me, darling, you fainted."

She glanced around the darkened room. "How did I get back here?"

"We brought you back."

She was dressed only in a cool cotton T-shirt and shorts. Neither of which belonged to her. "How did I get undressed?"

"Kate undressed you."

Alex stood and turned the ceiling fan to a higher speed. "How are you feeling?"

"Woozy. Why would I have fainted?"

"Heat exhaustion. Combined with no breakfast, lack of liquids and probably the stress from quitting smoking. You were a walking disaster just waiting to happen."

"But I had coffee this morning," Caris said. "Two cups."

"Caffeine dehydrates, especially in the heat. Drink this."

He helped her to sit, and waited until her dizziness passed before pressing a cool glass of water into her hand.

She drank deeply. Cold water had never tasted so wonderful.

Caris's cheeks burned, this time, from embarrassment and not heat. "I can't believe I fainted."

"You did," Alex said. He placed a cool hand on her forehead, making her shiver deliciously. "Your temperature seems almost back to normal. You should be fine in a day or so, as long as you take it easy."

"But I can't take it easy. I'm here to work."

"Are you always this difficult a patient?"

"No." She swung her legs over the side of the bed. "I'm sure I'll be fine once I get up..."

The room spun and Alex lowered her gently back onto the bed. "Care to take my word for it now?"

She couldn't even nod.

"You really need to take better care of yourself, Caris."

Funny, but that's exactly what her doctor kept telling her.

"It's not that easy, Alex. I have deadlines, negotiations, schedules to keep." She ticked off her responsibilities on one hand.

"And only one body. Screw that up and then see how far you get."

She stared at him, frustrated. "Why should you care so much?"

"Why should you care so little?"

She looked away.

Alex picked up her hand and squeezed it gently. "I'm worried about you."

Caris pulled back, unnerved by his caring touch. "Don't be. I'm tough. My dad used to tell me I'd never break. I bounce."

Alex smoothed her hair away from her forehead with a touch so gentle it almost made her cry. "Even bouncing balls break if they're thrown hard enough."

She felt her throat constrict at the unexpected tenderness. "I'd rather not talk about this. Can we talk about something else?"

"What would you like to talk about?"

"The land deal."

Alex looked disappointed. "So we're back to business already?"

"Yes. Would you really cancel our deal just because Harrison wanted to move out the residents?"

"Yes."

"Why is it so important to you that they stay?"

Alex stared out the window at the pounding surf. "I grew up on this island. I know and love these people. Over the years, I've watched them move away, unable to make a living here. Meanwhile, tourists boated in from Galveston to dive around the sunken ships and coral reefs, taking from the beauty of Navarro Island, then shipping out without leaving anything in return.

"During the eighties, the oil boom brought new residents, but after the market topped out, they all moved, which left the island poorer than it had been before. I went to college, and ended up staying in New York working as a financial analyst on Wall Street."

Caris nodded. She knew about that part of Alex Navarro's life.

"But I never stopped thinking of this island as my home. After my father died, I came back, and..." He shrugged. "I just want to help the island get back on its feet again, and this seems like the best way to do it."

Alex turned to her. His expression hardened, and before her eyes he turned into the tough negotiator she'd read about in *Fortune.* "If Harrison thinks he can depose these people, I'll cancel the deal without a qualm."

"Harrison won't do that."

Alex arched an eyebrow. "How can you be so sure? He's said that's what he plans to do."

"No. He won't do it."

"How do you know that?"

When she looked at him, she felt the heavy mantle of responsibility that Alex wore ease onto her shoulders. The islanders couldn't have picked a better guardian for their future. "Because you won't let him."

Alex pressed his lips against the palm of her hand, and she caught her breath. He smiled at her, his big hand still holding hers.

They stayed that way, with only their hands touching, for a long time.

9

IT WAS JUST PAST NINE that night when Caris stepped out of the shower and heard a knock on her bedroom door. "Just a minute." She gathered her terry-cloth robe around herself and belted it tightly.

She skipped to the door, hoping it was Alex again. Earlier, he'd brought her more chewing gum and spent most of the afternoon playing Monopoly with her. The activity had helped keep her mind off cigarettes and the morning's embarrassing fainting spell.

"Oh, it's you."

Harrison stood in the doorway, sneering down his patrician nose at her. "And who exactly were you expecting?"

"I'm sorry, Harrison. I'm still not myself yet," she lied, reminding herself that she was speaking to the man who held her professional future in his hands.

"That's what I wanted to talk to you about," Harrison said, coming into her room.

Caris closed the door and leaned against it. She crossed her arms, feeling vulnerable in her robe, wishing it was a business suit instead.

"I'll make this quick," Harrison said. "I've been concerned about your behavior, Caris."

"*My* behavior? Harrison, if this is about my fainting this morning, I'm fine, really..."

He held out his hand, halting her speech. "It's not about your illness, Caris. It's about you and Navarro."

Her heart skipped a beat. "Me and Alex?"

Harrison frowned. "Are you going to repeat everything I say?"

She felt herself blush. "No. Go ahead, Harrison."

Harrison picked up a piece of sugary bubble gum from the nightstand, examined it, then replaced it. "I figured this would happen if a female came as my partner on this trip."

The way Harrison pronounced it, female was a dirty word.

"Is there something you don't like about my work, Harrison? If so, tell me and I'll rectify it."

"It's not your work that I'm concerned about, Ms. Johnson. It's your hormones."

"My *hormones?*"

"Alex Navarro is a handsome man. I'll grant you that. But I hoped you'd be professional enough to keep your panties on until this deal is completed and we return to Washington."

My panties?

"After the deal is done," Harrison said, "you're on your own. I don't care if you sleep your way through the entire country. But until Alex Navarro signs the merger with Harrison, Harrison, Joffrey and Peters, I expect you to act like a lady."

A lady?

"And just what, exactly, have I been acting like?" Caris asked, amazed that her calm voice didn't mimic the screaming incredulity she felt inside.

Harrison lifted one eyebrow. "I'd tell you, but I prefer not to use that kind of language in mixed company."

Caris reminded herself to count to ten. Twice. In two languages. "Harrison, whatever you think has gone on between Alex Navarro and me, I can assure you that we have done nothing improper."

Harrison picked up the chewing gum from the nightstand. "He's given you gifts."

"He gave me a piece of chewing gum, for Pete's sake!"

"He carried you to the car."

"I was unconscious!"

Harrison shook his head. "If I had my way, you'd be on the next plane to D.C."

She tightened her jaw. "So why aren't I?"

He put the chewing gum back on the nightstand. "Because for some unknown reason, Martin Joffrey sees your work as invaluable."

The underlying hostility in Harrison's voice was obvious. His reasoning wasn't.

"You don't see my work as valuable?" Caris asked.

Harrison shrugged. "I'm sure Mr. Joffrey's seen more of it than I have."

"I'm not asking you about any of the work I've done in the past. I'm asking you about my work on Navarro Island. With you."

He glared at her. "Precisely."

Caris was confused. What was Harrison talking about?

Suddenly, she understood. Rumor abounded at the law firm that this land deal was Harrison's last chance to prove himself to the other partners. If he failed, Joffrey would force him into early retirement.

No wonder Harrison didn't trust her. He thought she was Joffrey's spy.

Relief rushed through Caris like a warm ocean current. Harrison's hostility and disparaging comments hadn't had anything to do with her skill as a lawyer. It was all a simple misunderstanding.

If they could settle their differences, Caris knew she and Harrison would both profit. Working together, the land deal was bound to go through. Harrison would return to the law firm a hero.

Caris would return a full partner.

She grinned. This was one of those win-win situations. No one would lose. Not even Alex Navarro or the people of Navarro Island.

"Harrison, I think I know what's going on."

Harrison frowned, the skin on his sunburned forehead puckering. "Of course you know what's going on, Caris."

"You don't understand—"

"I understand perfectly."

"No. You don't. Listen to me, Harrison."

"I don't need to listen to you, Caris. I know what's going on." He wagged an imperious finger at her. "I won't have your extracurricular activities sullying my reputation."

Her lips quivered. "Excuse me?"

"You heard me. If you can't manage to keep your panties on, I'll have no choice but to recommend termination upon our return to D.C."

"But, you don't understand—"

"I understand perfectly," he repeated. "I should never have allowed Joffrey to talk me into taking a female on this trip."

"Now, wait one minute—"

Harrison turned toward the door, dismissing her with an arrogant shake of his pink, balding head. "Watch yourself, Caris. You're not as necessary as you think."

He closed the door behind him.

Caris curled her fingers into a tight fist and stifled a scream. To think she'd actually imagined that she and Harrison could help each other. What a pompous jerk!

Caris had sacrificed her entire life for her law career. She'd subdued her femininity to fit in among the "big boys" at the law firm. All Harrison had to do to become partner was be born.

Now Harrison had the nerve to accuse her of acting like a slut.

She hadn't had a physical relationship with a man in over eight years. As a matter of fact, until Alex, she hadn't even been kissed by a man since the office Christmas party two years ago when one of the law interns had cornered her under the mistletoe.

Caris paced the room furiously. Male lawyers could act as they wanted, sleep with whomever they wanted, and their co-workers turned a tolerant and blind eye. Yet if a woman even smiled at a man, she was a slut.

A slut! She laughed at the irony.

And with Alex Navarro of all people.

She continued to pace furiously.

Sure, she was attracted to Alex Navarro, and his kisses packed a hell of a sexual wallop, but that didn't mean she had any intention of sleeping with him. She was a professional attorney, skilled in rational debate, not some immature teenager with raging hormones and inadequate impulse control.

Caris tugged at her bun, feeling her scalp itch and pull.

I have to get out of here.

She tore through the clothing in the bureau, looking for her swimsuit, thinking of swimming back to the mainland, or at the least, expelling some energy before she exploded.

She found the red bikini.

Why not?

She threw her bathrobe to the floor and slid into the bathing suit. If Harrison thought she was a slut, she might as well dress like one.

Caris raced out the door and down to the pounding surf. She dived in, barely aware of the warm water as it sluiced its way over her skin.

Her strokes were steady and sure as she swam away from shore. She immersed herself in the rhythm of her movements. Indignant rage fueled her progress.

Something grabbed her arm in the darkened sea and tugged. Caris screamed.

"Relax. It's just me. Alex."

She stared at him, her eyes filled with tears of outrage.

"Caris, what is it?"

"I've had it! I gave my life to that damned company and

now they..." She emitted an outraged grunt. Words couldn't describe what she was feeling.

"It's all right, Caris." Alex scissored his legs to stay near her. He stroked her arm softly. She trembled. "When I saw you swimming so vigorously I thought you'd decided to swim back to Texas for a cigarette," he said in a teasing voice.

She wanted to smile, but her lips were numb with emotion.

"What's wrong, Caris?"

She pulled her arm away. "What *isn't* wrong?"

She turned to swim away but he clamped his hands on her bare hips, holding her back.

"Let go of me!"

He held on. She stopped struggling, allowing her tense body to sink into the water and settle against him. Her heart pounded fiercely as his body finally touched hers, but her anger was too strong to be overcome.

"You can let go of me, Alex. You've proved your point. You're stronger than me." She kept her tone icy; it was the voice of the formal lawyer he'd met at the airport a few days ago.

He released her but stayed close enough to grab her if she tried to swim away. "I wasn't trying to prove anything, Caris. I just don't want you to get hurt."

She whirled. "What is it with you men? When *you* swim out to sea, you're called an athlete, yet when a woman does it, she's considered a danger to herself. Why is there always a double standard?" She slapped the water with her fist, splattering him. "Men!"

He grabbed her fist and squinted through sea-wet lashes. "Can we finish this conversation on dry land? I may be a man, but I'm not comfortable so far from shore."

Caris looked toward the distant shore. "I didn't realize I had swum so far."

She took off for land at a furious pace, her arms slicing

through the water, conquering it. Out of the corner of her eye, she saw Alex strain to catch up with her. Gradually, they began to swim in rhythm.

Caris's pace slowed subtly as she ran out of the anger that had been fueling her. In its place was a frustrating sense of the inevitable. As they neared shore, Caris turned and floated on her back, closing her eyes.

It was futile trying to fit into Harrison's world. No matter how much she conformed to his rules, she would never be accepted. She would always be considered a woman, an outsider, an inferior.

Caris took a shuddering breath and swiped at eyes wet with tears.

"Do you want to talk about it?" Alex asked.

"No." She drew her hands through the water slowly, savoring its unusual texture. "I can't go back, Alex." She heard the desperation in her voice and it scared her.

"You don't have to go back if you don't want to, Caris. You're a good lawyer. You can get a job anywhere."

Her anger surged. He thought she was upset about her *job*? She was upset about her *life*. She stood, balling her hands into fists. "I don't care about my job, Alex. Why should I? They don't care about me. All they care about is how much money I can make them." With a vicious tug, she pulled her hair free from what was left of its bun.

She dragged her fingers through her hair fiercely. "I gave up my whole life for them, Alex. And for what?"

"What made you so angry?" he asked softly.

Sudden, unexpected grief surged over her and she bit her lip to keep from crying out. "I want so much, Alex."

"So take it," Alex said gruffly.

The emotional intensity of his voice surprised her. "What?"

"You've gone after everything you've ever wanted, Caris. Why should this be so different?"

She stared at him.

"What do you want, Caris?"

Alex's wet torso gleamed golden in the moonlight and thoughts of the private life she'd sacrificed to her career taunted her.

She wanted to be happy. She wanted to be fulfilled. She wanted a man who would love and accept all the different sides of her: the business side with the leather briefcase and law briefs, and the female side with soft, sexy lingerie and aching kisses that went on forever.

She wanted Alex.

She shivered, standing on the verge of a new life.

"You, Alex. I want you."

The blatant desire in Alex's gaze made her heart race.

Empowered, Caris slid her hands up from the sea. Her fingertips skimmed across his flat stomach like a path of fire. She felt him quiver under her touch.

"Alex..." She brushed her wet hands over his nipples.

"Caris..."

She slid her hands to his shoulders, grasping them tightly. But still he held back. Desire flared in Caris. She wanted to taste him, devour him until they became one living, fluid being always together. She kissed his neck, licking drops of salty water from his skin.

His hands slid to her back and she shivered. With one touch, Alex had claimed her.

His hardened shaft brushed against the softness of her belly and she moaned.

"I want you, Alex."

Alex pulled away, his hands on her back the only thing holding her upright. She swayed, chilled and disoriented by his abrupt withdrawal. "Alex?"

"We shouldn't do this."

Her stomach constricted. She felt sick.

He doesn't want me.

The pain of his rejection overpowered even her embarrassment.

The only man I've ever truly wanted doesn't want me.

She wished she could drop into the ocean and disappear.

"You don't want me."

"It's not that, Caris. Of course I want you."

She couldn't look at his eyes. Couldn't bear to see his lies. "I know I'm not very experienced at this. I never meant to bother you..." She stepped back, shrinking with uncertainty.

Alex muttered a curse and hauled her into his arms, kissing her with a fierceness that startled her. His body warmed, soothed and excited her at the same time. She ached to be nearer to him.

Caris molded herself to his body, wrapping her arms and legs around him. Desire, only a flickering flame earlier, erupted like a volcano inside her.

When Caris had kissed Alex moments ago, it had been rage that had invigorated her, making her bolder than she'd ever been. She had been determined to enjoy the pleasure Harrison had already accused her of taking.

But she'd never expected to feel this.

When had the white heat of anger blazed into an even bolder red heat of desire? When had she started to tremble, not from rage, but from arousal?

When had she lost control, when all she ever really wanted was to be in control?

Alex pulled back, breathing heavily. Caris swayed in his embrace. His arms tightened around her, supporting her. For once, Caris was grateful to find someone stronger than herself to lean on.

"Does that feel like I don't want you?" He asked in a gruff voice.

Her brain felt as though it were wrapped in warm, liquid cotton. She didn't want to think, didn't want to talk. She wanted to be held, and loved—surrounded by Alex's arms, his body and this exotic lethargy of desire.

"If you want me and I want you then why don't we...?" She could feel herself blushing and hoped moonlight would hide it. Some femme fatale she was. She couldn't even say the words aloud.

"Not like this," Alex said, lowering her until her feet touched the sandy bottom. "I don't want you in my bed because you want to prove something to Harrison and the men at your law firm."

"But I don't—" She dropped her gaze, knowing he was right.

"Anger makes a lousy bedfellow, Caris," Alex said grimly. "Take it from someone who's been there."

"But that was before," Caris said. "Now it's different."

He stroked the small of her back. "You're still angry at Harrison."

"Yes, but that's only because he was wrong..." Caris's voice trailed off as she stared into Alex's eyes. In the moonlight, his eyes were the color of sweet chocolate.

"What was he wrong about?" Alex asked.

"About—"

In a flash Caris realized that Harrison wasn't wrong. He had seen the relationship developing between Caris and Alex and had known where it was headed.

Straight to Alex's bedroom.

She pulled away.

"What's wrong, Caris?"

"Nothing, I..." She moved her fingers through the water, drawing lazy patterns in the ocean, wishing she could design the future as easily as a few waves in the water.

What am I doing? I can't make love to this man. It will ruin everything. My career, my future, all my plans.

Alex placed one finger on her shoulder. His touch was so gentle Caris knew it shouldn't bring the banked inferno inside her back to life. But it did.

Alex placed a chaste kiss on her forehead. His kiss was so soft Caris knew it couldn't leave its mark like a brand on her soul. But it did.

Right or wrong, Alex was destined to be her lover. Her body had known it all along. Apparently, so had Harrison.

But what about Alex? She gazed at him. Did he feel it, too? This heat that incinerated all other thoughts but their bodies entwined in ecstasy?

Alex's hands shook slightly as he brushed her wet hair from her face. "We would have been great together." His voice trembled with regret.

Years of loneliness writhed inside Caris, taunting her. Her natural sensuality, bound in business suits and hairpins for so many years, rose to the surface.

There was no way she *couldn't* make love to Alex. He was her destiny. Far more than any law career would ever be.

The clarity of her decision made her shiver.

Caris leaned forward and pressed her lips to his with a confidence born of this understanding. She devoured his sensual groan and gave him one of her own.

"You know what will happen if they find out," Alex warned.

He was giving her one last chance to change her mind. Caris took a deep breath, inhaling the scent of the ocean. The scent of Alex.

Whatever happened to her job, whatever happened to her partnership, whatever happened to Navarro Island, Caris knew that Alex was destined to be her lover. She abandoned herself to that knowledge, reveling in the joy that came with giving up control.

"I want you, Alex."

"No regrets?"

"No regrets." For the first time in a very long time, Caris knew she was doing what she wanted to do.

"Turn around," Alex whispered huskily.

Her smile faltered. Years of battling for control warred with her newfound desires. "Why?"

Alex placed his hands on her shoulders and pressed gently until she turned away from him.

"What are you doing?" She twisted her head so she could watch him.

He pressed a warm, wet kiss on the back of her shoulder. "Relax."

"I don't relax very easily, Alex, I— Oh..."

Caris gave a breathy gasp as Alex tugged on her bikini string, releasing her from its confines.

He placed one hand under the curtain of her hair and lifted it, exposing her neck to the wet breeze. She giggled as he nibbled on the back of her neck.

Alex grasped the remaining bikini string with his teeth and pulled. Her bikini top slid into the ocean.

"I've been wanting to do that since I watched you run to the ocean. Now, turn around."

Caris did as he asked, thinking for the first time that maybe it wasn't so bad not to be the one in control. Her insides skittered with nervous anticipation as she wondered what he was going to do next.

"My God, Caris. You're beautiful." Although his gaze never left her face, Caris knew that Alex was seeing all of her. Not just her physical appearance, but everything about her.

"I am?"

"Oh, yes." He bent his head slowly and licked one pert nipple. Caris threw her head back, arching her body toward him, needing more than she could ever put into words.

When he pulled away, Caris moaned a protest.

"I want you, Caris."

Caris held out her arms. "Yes, Alex."

Alex put one arm behind her back. He bent suddenly, startling her. His other arm slipped under her knees. Caris gasped when he lifted her out of the water and into his arms. She threw her arms around his neck, holding him tightly.

As Alex carried her the final yards toward land, Caris showered kisses on his lips, his jaw, his shoulder. Anywhere she could reach. Her hands roamed over him, discovering him, claiming him.

Alex stood outside his bedroom door and gazed at her with an honest need she found humbling. "Do you really want this, Caris? Once we go inside, I'm not letting you go."

She tightened her arms around his neck. "I don't want you to let me go, Alex."

He dipped his head, claiming her with an urgent kiss, then strode quickly into the room.

Caris shivered as Alex nudged the bedroom door closed with his bare foot. Her gaze never left his as he lowered her feet to the floor until she was standing before him. Her stomach twitched with nervousness. And arousal.

Alex ran his hands up her back, leaving a trail of shivering need. She closed her eyes as desire rolled over her like a tidal wave.

He nibbled her neck. She sighed. He kissed the soft skin of her stomach. She moaned. The rough cotton sheets scraped her back in a sensitive massage.

When had she decided to lie down on the bed?

Caris closed her eyes and gave herself over to the surge of arousal Alex's lips and hands created.

She felt her bikini bottom being eased down her legs. She should be overwhelmed by how quickly things were moving, but everything felt so right. There was no turning back.

But Caris didn't want to turn back. Not if it meant leaving Alex.

He trembled before her eyes, shaking with desire Caris knew was only for her. Her gaze wandered over him, lingering at his erection straining against the black cloth of his swimsuit. Caris's mouth went dry. The thought of joining with this man left her weak with wanting. Trembling, Caris held out her arms.

Eagerly, Alex came to her, folding her into the heat of his embrace. With a reverence that made her want to cry, he touched her.

He nuzzled her earlobe. When he bit her gently, his warm breath shivering across her ear, she gasped.

Alex kissed her, teasing her with the gentleness of his touch. With unsteady hands, Caris grabbed his head and pulled him closer, melding his mouth to hers. She wanted to be so close to him that, when he exhaled, she received air.

She inhaled deeply. The scent of salt and desire made her head tingle deliciously.

Alex's weight on her was solid and welcome. She parted her thighs, feeling him press against her.

"Take them off." She moaned, hating the briefs that stood between her and ecstasy. She slid a finger beneath the elastic band of his swimsuit, and with her other hand caressed the smooth curve of his back.

"Not yet, Caris," he murmured, kissing his way down her neck. "I've wanted you for so long I don't want it to be over too quickly."

She inhaled sharply as his tongue licked a path down her neck straight to one wet, rigid nipple.

"You taste like the sea," he murmured.

"Is that good?" She felt oddly insecure.

His laugh was softer than his touch. "It's wonderful. You feel like liquid fire in my arms."

Stretching languorously, Caris felt more powerful than she ever had in a business suit.

His hand burned its way to her core.

"Oh, Alex!" She arched her back off the bed.

Pulling back to look at her, his eyes devoured her.

She felt unsure suddenly, afraid she didn't compare with the women Alex must have known. Her hands fluttered nervously. "Alex, I—"

"Don't, Caris," he whispered, kissing her hands away. "You are the most beautiful woman I have ever seen. Let me look at you."

A spurt of unfamiliar wickedness shot through her as feminine confidence overcame her insecurity. "What if I want to look at you?"

His look was as potent as a kiss and he peeled his swimsuit off.

He licked the inside of her thigh.

Overwhelmed by the sensation of his lips on her sensitive skin, Caris gasped.

With his tongue, he patiently tended the fire inside her, building it to a roaring inferno.

He pulled away suddenly, leaving her gasping, so close to the explosion. Frustrated, she groaned and reached for him. "Alex!"

"Just a moment, Caris." She heard the sound of a wooden drawer scraping open. When he returned, he was ripping open a foil packet with his teeth.

He pulled her into his arms and Caris forgot about everything but her need for this strong, dark man.

The hair on his thighs brushed against her, scratching an itch she'd never even known existed until tonight.

Slowly, he rotated his hips, torturing her with his patience.

"Alex, please…" She wrapped her legs around him, holding him prisoner in her embrace, fire raging inside her.

He licked her ear, making her shiver. His voice was husky with desire. "Tell me what you want, Caris. Tell me how to please you."

He moved again and she cried out, overrun with pleasure. "You, Alex. I want you… I need you."

Alex groaned and buried himself in her. He nibbled on her neck, his teeth creating a pleasurable torture.

But she wanted more.

"Alex, please…"

Her hands on his back, she undulated her hips, using her body to tell him what she wanted.

Tension spiraled inside her until it exploded in a roar, burning away all her tension, her fear, her loneliness. She heard Alex moan and cry out, consumed by the heat of her inferno.

Afterward, they held each other, warmed by the burning embers of their passion.

CARIS AWOKE with a start. She looked around the dark room and panicked. She had no idea where she was. Her body felt strange and heavy. There was an odd warmth between her thighs.

The warmth twitched and awareness shot through her. Her stomach sank, a mixture of excitement and panic.

Alex lay asleep beside her, his face open and trusting in the moonlight. One arm was flung over his head, the other lay between her thighs, his hand cupping her, even in sleep, claiming her.

Caris lay back against the bed.

What had she done? She, a woman who always considered the consequences of each and every action, had never even considered the possibilities of making love with Alex. If Alex hadn't taken precautions, they could have conceived a child. Then what would have happened to her future?

Her insides warmed with a sudden, unexpected tenderness at the thought of Alex's child growing in her. A piece of him always with her. For a second, she almost wished he hadn't considered the consequences, either. *Almost.* But then reality intruded.

What have I done?

Old Mr. Harrison, the first founding partner of the firm, was probably rolling over in his grave this very minute as he watched the scene from above.

Well, knowing old Mr. Harrison as she had, he was probably watching from below.

No sense thinking about that now. She had to think about how to get out of here before Alex woke up.

And before anyone else found out what she had done.

ALEX FELT Caris pull away from him long before she tried to disentangle his hand from the warmth of her thighs.

He knew what she was thinking, knew she probably regretted giving in to the impulse that had landed her in his arms last night. Any good lawyer would be assessing damage control.

But not Alex.

Alex felt nothing but satisfaction, and a wholeness inside where before had only been a gaping cavern.

No matter what Caris Johnson thought, this night was far from over.

CARIS MANAGED to move Alex's hand to the edge of her thigh, when he stretched, making her quiver with more than embarrassment.

His hand felt so foreign, and yet so right against her. As much as she was enjoying his touch, Caris knew that she had to get out of this room. Quickly. She glanced through the window at the brightening sky. The sun would be up soon. Unless she left now, someone could see her scurrying away from Alex's room.

Caris held her breath and gingerly placed her hands around Alex's wrist. She glanced at his sleeping visage, then pulled his hand slowly upward.

"Good morning."

Caris shrieked in surprise and dropped Alex's hand back into her lap.

He leaned over and kissed her full on the mouth, the dark stubble of his beard scraping her chin in a way she was surprised to find she liked. She kissed him back, her mind whirring like a small engine, drowning out all background noise.

Come on, Caris. Are you really prepared to give up everything you've worked for just for a roll in the hay?

Caris gasped as her conscience nudged her. She pulled away, wishing she could erase the pleasurable tingles coursing through her body.

"You're even more beautiful this morning than you were last night." Alex moved to kiss her again.

Caris pulled away. "Alex, we have to talk."

He frowned and her fingers ached to rub the furrow between his eyebrows that her words had created.

She suddenly realized she was naked and lying in bed with her potential corporate partner. She plucked his hand off her thigh and stepped out of bed as nonchalantly as she could manage. She tried to pretend she was used to parading around naked in front of her lover.

Her lover.

It was such a nice way to describe Alex.

Caris ordered herself not to weaken. She pulled Alex's bathrobe off the door hook and huddled into it. It was too long and far too big, so she sat in the rocking chair near the bed, curled her legs under her and wrapped the robe around herself like a blanket.

"We need to talk, Alex," she repeated. Caris took a deep breath.

Big mistake.

His scent clung to the robe, tantalizing her hunger more than the smell of baking bread the day after she'd started a diet.

Alex leaned against the headboard and folded his arms across his flat stomach. She stared at the arrow of hair flaring across his belly and lower.

"You wanted to talk, so talk." The anger in his voice surprised her.

"Why are you angry?" she asked.

"Do you really have to ask?"

"I don't understand…"

Alex took a deep breath. "What did you want to tell me, Caris?" Although he was still angry, his voice was soft, and unsettled her more than if he'd yelled.

Caris was surprised to find herself more nervous than her first day in court. "This was a mistake."

He glared at her. *"That's* why I'm so angry, Caris."

She frowned. Did Alex regret what had happened last

night also? Although she'd been prepared to sacrifice last night's experience for the good of her career, it hurt to see Alex dismissing it. Hadn't their lovemaking meant anything to him? It had meant everything to her.

She bit her lower lip. She would not cry. At least not in front of him.

She should be grateful, she told herself. Their affair was over. There would be no complications, no recriminations, nothing to get in the way of her partnership. They could simply pretend that last night never happened.

It's for the best.

If that was true, why did she want to weep?

Caris forced a bright smile, determined not to let Alex see how hurt she was. "So we're in agreement, then. Good."

Alex shook his head. "We're not in agreement, Caris."

"We're not? But I thought— Exactly why are you angry?"

Alex sighed. "I'm angry because you think last night was a mistake."

Her heart skipped a beat and hope made her dizzy. "And you don't?"

"I've made a lot of mistakes in my life, Caris, but this was definitely not one of them."

Alex slid out of bed and walked toward her, showing no concern for his nudity. Caris forced herself not to stare at the highlights and shadows the dawn painted across his hard body.

"And I'm going to prove it to you."

10

"I DON'T WANT THIS!" Caris jumped out of the rocking chair. Although her jaw was tightly defiant, Alex could see the uneasiness flickering in her green eyes. She tightened the belt of the robe in a protective gesture.

Alex folded his arms over his bare chest and stood in front of her. "What do you want, Caris?"

Caris blinked rapidly against a growing sheen of tears. "I don't know what I want."

"Do you want to know what I want?" Alex asked.

Caris nodded, her gaze furtive, as though she feared what he was about to say.

"I want you, Caris."

"But you can't have me!" Her voice rose to a shriek. "Not like this!" She paced, the edge of the robe almost tripping her. "Why did I ever have to do this?"

"Caris, it's all right. I won't force you to do anything you don't want to."

"Don't you see, Alex?" She turned to face him. "I wanted you. I still want you. Oh, God." She buried her face in her hands.

"So what's the problem?"

"What isn't the problem?" Caris wailed. "I can't have sex with you."

"You already did."

Caris balled the edges of the robe inside her fist, frustration evident on her face. "I know that! I meant, I can't do it again."

Alex smiled.

"This isn't funny! I'm upset!"

And she was. Alex could see it. "Tell me what you want, Caris, and if it's within my power, I'll do it."

Caris's lips quivered. "Last night shouldn't have happened, Alex."

His stomach sank. "But it did happen, Caris. We can't change that."

"I know we can't. But we can pretend it never happened."

How could she deny what had happened between them last night? It was what Alex had been searching for his whole life. A sudden suspicion teased him. Had Caris slept with him only to gain control of the merger?

No. Caris couldn't be that cold-blooded. Could she? He had to know for sure.

"Why did you sleep with me, Caris?"

Her cheeks turned pink and she shrugged, looking young and lost, her body enveloped in his big robe. "I don't really know why, Alex."

He knew the truth then. Knew that whatever had happened between them last night, Caris had not designed it. Last night had been an act of passion, not avarice. He wanted to kiss her in relief but suspected if he did, she'd bolt.

Alex knew Caris was afraid. Not of him, but of herself. Last night, she hadn't been the logical attorney she claimed to be, but the sensual woman she'd almost forgotten. And that scared Caris senseless.

But Alex had never gotten anywhere by being timid. He took a step toward her. "I know why you stayed with me."

"You do?" Caris shrank away from him, but it wasn't fear that lurked in the gaze that darted over his body. It was desire. Her gaze skimmed over his body as softly as a kiss.

"You've denied your feelings too long, Caris, and last night they demanded to be heard. Demanded to be held." He stood before her, waiting until she finally looked into his eyes. "Demanded to be loved."

He touched her cheek softly and she quivered.

He waited for her kiss with tremulous anticipation.

But she didn't kiss him.

"Last night wasn't about love, Alex. It was about sex."

Her voice was cold, but before Alex could feel the pain of those words, he heard the doubt in her voice. Her words lacked the ring of conviction. Caris was lying, trying to convince him that their lovemaking meant nothing to her. It was a statement designed to hurt him, designed to push him away. Alex tightened his jaw. He wasn't going anywhere. And neither was she.

"What do you want from me, Caris?"

She laughed hollowly. "Apparently, I've already taken it."

So that was how she was going to play it. Cool, tough, the experienced flirt, when he already knew how inexperienced she really was. Two could play at that game, and Alex definitely had the advantage.

But Caris had his heart.

"You have to admit," Alex said teasingly, "it was great sex."

Caris stepped away from him, her gaze downcast. "I needed you last night, Alex, but it was because I needed to be touched. And you—" she shrugged and turned to face him, her expression once again the controlled mask of the attorney he'd met four days ago at the airport "—you were convenient, Alex."

If he believed her, it would hurt. Luckily, he didn't.

"Look me in the eyes and tell me that, Caris."

"I just did." But her gaze remained focused somewhere around his chin.

"Tell me more," Alex said.

"What more do you want?"

She sounded panicked and Alex willed himself not to smile. He'd called Caris's bluff and she had no other plan to fall back on.

He had won. Of course, not completely. Caris still hadn't told him she loved him.

"Tell me more about the sex," Alex said.

Caris's blush rose from the inside of the robe and he knew she was blushing all over. He wished it was him, and not merely his clothing, touching her, being warmed by that heat.

"Alex, really, I don't think that—"

"Humor me." His voice was quiet but authoritative. Kate had once told him his voice could reduce a person to tears if used in that way.

Caris barely even wobbled. She glared at him. "How graphic do you want me to get?"

This is going to be fun.

"Very graphic."

Alex grinned, a ruthless, diabolical grin, and Caris knew she was lost. She tugged at her unbound hair, wishing she had some bobby pins to tame it. She felt lost, disoriented, like a country mouse wandering unescorted in New York's subway system. Why had she ever made love with Alex?

Because she had wanted to. Alex had touched her in a place she had almost forgotten she had—her heart.

Again, the reality of her actions overwhelmed her and panic rose. She had to get out of here. Caris began to pace. The robe slipped and she jerked at it, wishing she was anywhere but here.

That's a lie, she admitted. She really wanted to be in that bed. With Alex. Naked and not saying a word.

Her gaze drifted to the bed, appraising the wordless road map their bodies had made of the sheets.

If she got back in that bed, she might never leave it. And then where would she be?

She took a deep breath. The only way she was going to get out of this room was if she made Alex hate her.

But the only way she could do that was to hurt him.

Her stomach tightened at the thought of hurting Alex. But what else could she do?

"The sex was great," she said, grateful that her voice had

stopped shaking, although the rest of her body still shook like an earthquake. "You really know your stuff, Alex. You must have had a lot of practice."

"Practice," Alex murmured, "but never the real thing."

Caris's knees buckled. Was Alex saying he loved her?

He was still staring at her, expecting more, and Caris knew she couldn't go on with this. No matter how much she wanted to get out of this room with her career still intact, she couldn't force herself to hurt Alex. She had to tell him the truth. At least part of it. "Come on, Alex. What do you want from me? It was wonderful, I'll admit it. But it was just one night. And that's all it will ever be."

"Why?"

The softness of his voice startled her. "Why what?"

"Why does it have to be only one night, Caris? Why can't it continue?"

"Come on, Alex. Be realistic. Do you honestly think it's a good idea for us to have a sexual relationship right now?" Her laugh sounded bitter even to her own ears. "Hormones aside, I couldn't have chosen a more inappropriate bed partner."

Alex eyed Caris with an expression she couldn't decipher. "I would never call what we shared last night inappropriate."

"Damn it, Alex! You've got to understand where I'm coming from. I'm involved in the most important deal of my life. If it goes well, I'm set. The fast track to a law partnership. I'll be in a place few lawyers, let alone female lawyers, even get to dream about. I can't throw it all away on a sexual escapade!"

"Is that all I was to you? A sexual escapade?"

She didn't want to answer that. "Look, Alex, I don't know about your company, but my law firm has certain standards. Sleeping with the competition isn't going to win me any points. If this gets out—"

"You'll lose everything," Alex said.

Good. He understood how important this was to her. "I need your word you won't talk about what happened last night."

"Caris, why would I talk about what happened between us? It was private."

She wanted to believe him, but years of ruthless competition made her wary. "So I have your word?"

"Why won't you trust me? For God's sake, Caris, last night we were as close as a man and woman can be."

Caris glanced at the bed, remembering how close, and how spectacular, they had been. She needed to leave before she did something stupid. Like kiss him. "It's not going to happen again."

"It's not?" Alex took a step toward her, the softness of his voice at odds with the determined gleam in his eyes.

"No, it's not. I—"

He swept her into his arms, kissing her, arousing every emotion she thought she'd subdued, and suddenly it didn't seem so important for her to be anywhere but where she was at that moment. In Alex's arms.

CARIS RETRIEVED her salt-stiff bikini bottom from Alex's bedroom floor. "This doesn't change anything."

He had the nerve to smile.

"Just because we made love again—"

"Twice," Alex interrupted, still smiling.

She felt like grinning, herself, but didn't allow it. "Just because we made love twice more doesn't mean that anything's changed."

She slipped into the bikini bottoms with a grimace, the dried sea salt scraping her tender flesh.

Alex lay on the bed, still smiling. The bedsheet was pooled at the foot of the bed, concealing nothing from her gaze. He patted the spot beside him. "Why don't you come back to bed? We have at least twenty minutes before the sun comes up."

"Tempting an offer as that is, no."

She slipped one of his T-shirts over her naked breasts. Her bikini top was lost, floating somewhere in the gulf.

If he kissed her, Caris knew she would stay. She prayed he stayed on the bed, away from her.

"What are you so afraid of, Caris?"

She winced as she ran a hand through her hair, now coated with sea salt and hopelessly tangled. "Losing my job, what else?"

"No, it's more than that. Are you afraid I'll take control of you somehow, subjugate you to my—"

"Could we skip the amateur psychotherapy?" Caris glared at him. He had stumbled a little too close to the truth for her comfort.

Alex raised his hands in mock defeat.

"Why is it so hard for you to accept that I'm afraid of losing my job?" Caris asked. "I don't see you advertising the fact that you're sleeping with the enemy."

"You're not my enemy, Caris. And besides, we haven't even left the room. If it will make you feel better, though, I'll take out an ad on national television. Right during the soap operas so we can be sure my sister sees it."

"All right, so you're not afraid of anything," she grumbled.

"I didn't say that. I said I'm not afraid of telling everyone I'm involved with you."

Caris felt the walls begin to close in on her.

If Alex told Harrison they were sleeping together, Harrison would fire her on the spot. She probably wouldn't even get plane fare back to D.C.

"Look, Alex, I—"

He was beside her suddenly, his movements so smooth they made her shiver.

With one hand, he pushed her hair away from her neck. Then he kissed her.

When she opened her eyes, he smiled. "Whatever you want to do is fine by me, Caris."

She shivered with relief.

"Thank you, Alex."

He kissed the tip of her nose. "Until this deal is over, Caris. Then all bets are off."

"What?"

He kissed her again, almost as though he couldn't help himself. "Until the merger goes through, you and I will act like two business acquaintances. I won't tell anyone about what happened here—" he nodded toward the bed "—and I'll follow whatever lead you plan to take."

She stared at the bed, wishing the sun wasn't about to rise, wishing she could be Caris Johnson, the lover, for a few more hours instead of returning to her business suits and hair combs and the lonely life of Caris Johnson, attorney-at-law.

"We keep our relationship out of the land deal, and act like professionals." Alex's hands smoothed her shoulders, caressing her tension away.

"What happens when it's over?" She steeled herself for his answer.

He kissed her again.

"After this deal is completed and all the paperwork is signed, I'm coming for you, Caris. And we're going to follow this relationship wherever it leads us."

"Why?"

He kissed her eyelids shut, his breathing labored, as though he was trying to absorb the scent of her. "Why?" His face barely touched the wisps of her hair. "Because nothing like this has ever happened to me before. And I'm willing to bet nothing like this has ever happened to you before, either."

Then he kissed her and it was a long time before she could pull herself from his arms and flee to her room, fearing she'd left the best thing in her life behind her.

CARIS WAS STILL SMILING as she slipped into a business suit after her shower. She felt relaxed. Her body hummed with pleasure.

She felt invincible.

Someone knocked on her door. Harrison pushed into the room. "I waited until a more reasonable hour to discuss this with you."

Caris glanced at the clock. It was 6:07 a.m. *This* was a more reasonable hour? Her body went cold. Hadn't he insulted her enough yesterday? Suddenly she felt clammy with fear. What if Harrison knew where she'd spent the night?

"What do you want, Harrison?"

"I've been thinking."

Caris gulped. "Yes?"

"About Alex Navarro." He paused and her heart sank.

He knew about her and Alex and he was merely toying with her, waiting for the right moment to attack, end her legal career for good.

"Yes?" She almost didn't want to know.

Harrison glared at her. "Don't you find it funny that Alex Navarro is looking for partners to develop this resort when he could do it himself?"

Her head spun. "What?"

"The merger," Harrison said.

"Is this about last night?"

Harrison waved her comment away. "I may have been out of line." He rolled his eyes. "Please, Caris, do try to concentrate on business."

Business? Harrison was talking about *business?* Caris almost fell over with relief. "Well, I..." What was it Harrison had asked her?

"The financial reports of Navarro Investments indicate a company wealthy enough to finance its own beach resort. So, why isn't Navarro doing it himself? Why bring us in?"

"He doesn't want to tie up his own capital," Caris said.

"Obviously, Caris, but wouldn't most people rather risk

their capital than give up so much control over a project? Especially a project as important as this one appears to be to Alex Navarro?"

"Perhaps it has something to do with his father's will," she said. "I'll call the office and see if the will is out of probate yet."

"No phones," Harrison said. "The man lives like a heathen."

"No phones? Are you sure, Harrison?" She could have sworn she'd seen a cellular phone next to her suitcase in the trunk of Alex's Land Cruiser.

"Of course I'm sure," Harrison replied testily. "Perhaps you should spend less time sleeping and more time thinking about your job."

"Well, I..." Her voice trailed off. Harrison was staring at her. "What?"

Harrison's gaze slithered over her. "You look different."

She glanced in the mirror. Oh, God. She *did* look different. She was positively radiant and the frown lines she'd had since law school were gone. "My hair is down," she said, hoping that was the only difference the senior partner had noticed.

"That must be it." Harrison finally turned away. "Think about that business with Navarro and let me know if you come to any conclusions."

Caris closed the door behind Harrison, her knees shaking. That was too close.

She leaned closer to the mirror. If this was what love could do to a woman's appearance, she should patent it and make a million dollars.

Love? Caris clapped a hand over her mouth. She couldn't be in love, and especially not with Alex Navarro, no matter how good a lover he was.

Her gaze softened and her limbs melted into puddles of pleasure at the thought of him.

Oh, no! She did look different, even when she just thought about him. Now what was she going to do?

She couldn't spend the rest of this business trip melting every time she even thought of the man. Someone was bound to notice. And Harrison, who only had suspicions now, would get verifiable proof. And then where would she be?

Out on her butt, without even a recommendation.

She had to do something, but what?

Give him up.

Caris's heart sank. How could she give Alex up? She didn't know for sure that she loved him, but she did know that she loved the way she felt whenever she was around him, and she loved all the things he did for her, and she loved...

Oh, Lord! Again, Caris caught sight of herself in the mirror, her face as soft as a lover's kiss. She was in trouble. Even thinking about Alex was reducing her to an incoherent puddle of emotion.

She had to fight this. And the only way she could do that was to keep Alex as far away from her as possible, at least until the merger was completed. Then, afterward, they would be free to pursue their relationship as far as they wanted to. And to hell with the consequences.

But until then, she and Alex were back to being adversaries.

11

ALEX ENTERED the dining room, his nostrils flaring from the sweet smell of rich coffee and homemade blueberry pancakes.

"I knew I hired you to be my butler for a reason, John." He patted his friend on the back.

"You hired me because I was free," John said, minus his British accent. "And because I'm the only one you trust with the complete truth. How are negotiations going? Do they suspect anything?"

Alex grinned, remembering his evening with Caris. "So far, so good."

"I'm glad." John placed a plate of pancakes on the table.

Alex put a hand on his friend's arm. "You don't have to do that. There's no one else around."

"Keeps me in character," John said, adding a hefty British accent.

Alex whistled absently as he piled his plate with pancakes. His fork hovered as he noticed John staring at him. "What?"

"What aren't you telling me?"

A lot, but Alex wasn't about to confide that. "Nothing. Why?"

"You look too happy."

Alex laughed. "How can a person look too happy?"

"It's possible. You're doing it." He filled Alex's coffee cup then set the coffeepot back on the table. "If we can pull this off, we're going to save the island."

"I hope so." He bit into a pancake, remembering the taste of Caris.

"Any word about the will?"

"Not yet." Using the cellular phone he'd hidden in the trunk of his car, Alex had called his father's attorney in Houston earlier this morning and been told that the will was still in probate.

Alex's body tensed in sudden longing and he knew Caris had just entered the room.

"If that will be all, sir," John said in his clipped, British accent.

John exited, leaving Alex and Caris alone. Alex grinned and was striding toward her before he'd consciously decided to move.

"I missed you after you left," he said.

Caris didn't say anything. She nibbled worriedly on her bottom lip. Her gaze darted around the room in a manner that reminded Alex of a cornered animal.

"Are you all right, Caris?" He reached out to touch her.

Caris stuffed her hands in her skirt pockets. Alex felt as though she had slapped him.

"I'm fine. Why do you ask?"

Her voice was hurried, her breathing rapid and uneven and her gaze touched everything but him. He frowned. "You don't look all right." He leaned closer, his voice a whisper. "This isn't about last night, is it?"

She stepped away quickly, putting the large dining-room table between them. "I thought we agreed not to discuss that again." She stared at the table, her fingers playing with the decorative fringe of the tablecloth.

"We agreed not to discuss it with other people around. But we're alone now. Caris, I—"

"Good morning." Harrison strolled into the room, acting as though he owned the world and it had suddenly turned into solid gold. "I thought I smelled breakfast." He took a seat at the foot of the table.

You have rotten timing, Harrison, Alex wanted to say. Instead he said, "It sounds like you had a pleasant evening."

Harrison placed a napkin on his lap with an unfamiliar flourish. "I did, thank you. I don't know if it's the clean air, or perhaps the salt from the sea, but I feel marvelous. Last night, I slept better than I have in years."

Alex's gaze returned to Caris who was still playing with the edge of the tablecloth.

"Funny, but I feel drained all of a sudden," Alex murmured.

Caris's eyes were a startled green when she finally looked at him. If he didn't know better, he'd say she was afraid. But of what?

Alex had already given his word that he wouldn't reveal what had happened between them. Perhaps Caris was afraid he would go back on his word. If she knew him better, she'd know he had a better chance of waking up female one morning than breaking a promise he made to her.

Unfortunately, she didn't know him better. And she didn't seem willing to give him the benefit of the doubt.

John came in, carrying a plate of bacon, and Alex's stomach recoiled at the fatty, salty odor. He had just lost his appetite. He pushed his plate away.

Alex watched Caris's fingers on the tablecloth's fringe. Was she thinking about a cigarette, or something else? And why had she been so cold to him? What was going on in that lawyerly mind of hers?

"What would you like to do today?" Alex asked.

Harrison smiled coyly. "I know what *you* would like to do today."

Alex's stomach tightened. Did Harrison know about him and Caris? If so, that would explain Caris's attitude toward him. "And what do I want to do today, Harrison?" He kept his tone coolly challenging.

Harrison cocked his head quizzically. "Why, discuss other improvements for the island, of course."

"Oh, of course." Alex picked up his coffee cup, his fingers bypassing the fragile handle and curving around the smooth white porcelain. He stared at Caris, wishing his hands were smoothing their way around her pale curves.

"When should we begin?" Harrison asked.

"Kate is spending the morning with her son on the beach. I'd like her to sit in on our meetings."

"Why?" a voice said.

They all turned to see Michael standing in the doorway.

"Why what?" Alex asked.

"Why Kate, why now?" Michael sounded annoyed that he had to explain himself.

"Why not?" Alex said. "She owns one-third of Navarro Investments, as we both do. I thought it would be good for her to get more involved in the business."

"Kate?" Michael snorted. "Kate wouldn't know a good business decision if it bit her!"

Alex jumped out of his seat, grasped his brother's arm and propelled him in the direction of the door with a backward, "Excuse us, please."

"Let go of me!" Michael pulled his arm free.

Alex closed the door behind them before replying. "What the hell do you think you're doing?" His voice was dangerously low. "Why did you make a scene like that in front of Caris and Harrison?"

"Oh, please." Michael rolled his eyes toward the ceiling. "Don't try to tell me you're worried about what either of them think. You could roll over Harrison without even thinking. And I know you've already been to bed with that woman."

"What?" He grabbed Michael's arm again. "Where did you get that idea?"

"I'm not blind. Or stupid." Michael pulled his arm away. "Just look at her. She has the look of a well-loved woman. It doesn't take a genius to figure out who gave her that look."

If they were that obvious, it was no wonder Caris was worried about her career. "Whatever you think happened, Michael, it's none of your business."

"Aha! I knew it!" Michael grinned and jabbed Alex in the stomach, hard enough so it hurt. "So tell me. What's she like underneath all those business clothes?"

Alex shrank away from his brother. "This is not a subject for discussion, Michael. And for your information, she and I are merely business acquaintances."

Michael grinned. "None of my business associates wear red bikinis to our meetings." He winked. "And then lose them in the ocean."

A shaft of fear pierced Alex's side. "What are you talking about, Michael?"

"Don't worry, brother. Your secret is safe with me."

Brother. The only time Michael called him brother was when he wanted something.

"Michael, what do you—"

"Look, you've had your fun, Alex. You got the pretty lawyer in the sack, now dump her."

"Excuse me?"

"You heard me. It's stupid to merge with these lawyers when we can sell the beach outright and make a ton of money."

"And what will happen to all the people on the island if we just sell the land? Where will they live?"

Michael shrugged. "Who cares?"

"I care."

"Then you're a fool."

Alex clenched his fingers. "Watch it, Michael, or I'll—"

"You'll what?" Michael stepped forward, aggressively bumping his chest against Alex's. "Beat me up? Kill me? Disown me? What?"

Alex stepped back with a sigh. "We used to be close, Michael."

"No!" Michael leaped forward aggressively, jabbing one finger into Alex's chest. "We were never close, Alex. I idolized you and then you abandoned me. You left for college and you never came back."

"Michael, I had to go away. What did you expect me to do? Stay here forever?"

"Yes!" Michael shouted. He turned away. "Go away, Alex. And take your girlfriend with you!"

"Michael, wait!"

Michael raced out the front door, slamming it behind him. The house shook with the force.

Alex took several deep breaths then turned toward the dining room.

Caris was staring intently at her plate. Although Alex could only see the top of her head, he saw that her forehead burned with embarrassment.

"Quite a fight you two had, eh, Navarro?" Harrison said, eager as a dog sniffing blood.

Alex grimaced. "You know how brothers are." He sat at the table and toyed with his spoon. "I'm sorry you had to hear that." He spoke only to Caris.

"We know how family is, don't we, Caris." Harrison tapped Alex on the arm, a gesture that would have felt comforting coming from anyone but Harrison.

Caris murmured something noncommittal.

"Sounds like your brother is jealous," Harrison said.

"Excuse me?"

"About your relationship with this mysterious woman," Harrison said.

Alex heard Caris inhale sharply.

"Anyone I know?" Harrison asked, his gaze edging toward Caris.

Alex didn't know how to answer that. Just how loud had he and Michael been?

"You must have misunderstood, Harrison," Caris said, her voice choked with what Alex guessed was fear.

Harrison frowned. "I don't think so, Caris. After all, the conversation was quite loud."

Alex felt like kicking himself.

Better yet, he felt like kicking Michael.

"I'm sure Mr. Navarro would rather not discuss his private life," Caris said, her voice strained.

I'd like to talk about my private life, Alex thought. *But not with Harrison.*

"I didn't mean to intrude," Harrison said. "No offense was intended."

"It's all right." Alex tossed his napkin on the table. He stood. "We'll begin negotiations this afternoon. I'll see you both at noon in the library."

He turned and left quickly, knowing both of them were watching him walk away.

CARIS PACED HER ROOM, her gaze darting between the ocean view and the desk clock. It read 11:48. In another twelve minutes she would be expected to sit across from Alex and pretend to be nothing more than a business acquaintance. She would have to pretend he hadn't been her first lover in eight years, hadn't been only her second lover in her entire life...hadn't meant more to her than she could say.

Her pacing increased. She wanted a cigarette.

You'll be fine, she told herself. *Concentrate on your legal strategy. Concentrate on winning. Don't concentrate on how Alex's bare skin felt, so warm against yours, pulsing with life and vitality, filling you with heat.*

Her body tingled with remembered awareness.

I said, don't think about that!

Someone knocked on the door and Caris's stomach tightened with dread. She wasn't up to a conversation with anyone right now, especially Alex.

Michael pushed his way into the room. "Michael!"

"I need to talk to you."

"Look, I don't think this is such a good idea. I—"

"I know about you and Alex."

She didn't even bother to deny it. "What do you want, Michael?"

Michael laughed humorlessly. "Don't worry. I'm not going to blackmail you or anything. I just want to talk to you."

Caris closed the door and folded her arms protectively over her chest. "So talk."

Michael's eyes were the same color as Alex's, but somehow seemed much darker. A shiver of fear shimmied up her spine and she adopted the authoritative tone of voice she used in court to counteract that fear. "What do you want, Michael?" she repeated.

"What do you think I want, Caris? I want you to make sure this deal doesn't go through."

"Why?"

"Does it matter? You're either going to help me or you're not."

"I'm not." Caris straightened her back, trying to look more invincible than she felt.

Michael shrugged. "Even if I can help you?"

"This conversation is over, Michael." She opened the door.

Michael arched one aristocratic eyebrow. "Aren't you even curious as to what I'm talking about? There might be something in it for your firm."

She wondered what he wasn't saying. Caris closed the door. "You've got five minutes."

Michael picked up a stick of bubble gum lying on her nightstand—the bubble gum Alex had given her. She longed to rip it out of his hand.

"What if I told you that you could make a lot of money helping me?" Michael asked.

"I'd tell you your time is up."

He shook his head, looking disappointed in her. "Maybe I was wrong about you. Maybe you and my brother do belong together, always spouting off about allegiance and responsibility. What *century* do you think this is, Caris? We're living in an age of eat or be eaten, kill or be killed. I thought that you of all people realized that."

"What do you mean, me of all people?"

He smiled slyly and Caris realized Michael was one of those people who enjoyed the fight more than the actual win. "Why don't you tell me. *Ice Queen.*"

Ice Queen. Caris flinched at the nickname she hadn't heard since her last year of law school. At least not to her face. She forced herself to speak slowly and clearly, sensing that, unlike Alex, Michael couldn't see right through her.

"What's the bottom line, Michael?"

"Bottom line is I don't want this deal to go through."

"Why not?"

Michael grinned. "Maybe I want to make a name for myself. You know what they say, Caris. All's fair in love and business."

Caris swallowed. In the past, she would have agreed with him. Now, she wasn't so sure. "So because you don't want the land deal to go through you think I should sabotage it?"

"Just don't make it any harder for me to break it up." Michael tossed the stick of gum up in the air and caught it in the palm of his hand.

"What the hell are you talking about?"

"I'll spell it out for you. Harrison has been a loose cannon this entire trip. It's obvious that if the deal were left to only Alex and Harrison, it would fall through. Even with you here acting as a buffer, any failure will probably reflect on Harrison. With Harrison gone, your partnership is practically assured."

He was right. But it still didn't explain what he was doing here. "If any deal between Harrison and Alex doesn't stand a chance, why don't you just get rid of me?"

Michael cocked his handsome head. "Because I like you, Caris."

"*Like* me? Please, don't do me any favors, Michael."

Michael slammed the gum back onto the nightstand. "I'm trying to help you out, Caris. So you can leave the island with more than just the memory of your sexual adventure."

"That's it, Michael. Get out."

"I could have gone straight to Harrison with this," Michael said, not moving.

"He wouldn't have believed you." She counted on Alex's brother not seeing through her bluff.

"But if he did..." Michael chuckled. *"Boom."*

Caris shivered. She'd have been on a plane, headed back to D.C.—and worse.

"Get out, Michael."

"I'm going." Michael raised his hands as though in defeat, but she knew better.

"Why are you doing this, Michael? Alex is your brother."

"Alex hasn't been my brother for a long, long time."

His smile reminded her of that of a crocodile eyeing a slow swimmer, and she took great pleasure in slamming the door in his face.

Caris shivered. If Michael went to Harrison, her career would be over before it had even begun.

So what could she do? If she went to Harrison and told him about Michael, she'd have to tell him the whole truth and she wasn't ready to do that.

Alex deserved to know that his brother was planning on destroying the land deal. But how could she tell him and not her own boss? And what if Alex didn't believe her? Worse, what if Alex already knew and this was actually only a ploy to raise their bid?

She grasped her spinning head as the watch on her alarm beeped—11:55. It was time to face the firing squad, with no blindfold and no cigarette.

Oh, God.

ALEX STOOD ALONE in the library and poured himself a liberal dose of Johnnie Walker Black.

"You don't look too good."

He looked up to see his sister standing in the doorway, her cheeks flushed pink from her morning on the beach. "You look a lot better than you did last night," he said. He held out his arms and Kate burrowed into his open embrace. "Feeling better?"

She nodded against his shirt, then pulled back. "Thanks to you. I'm not sure why I got so weepy last night, except..."

"It's scary starting a new life," Alex finished for her. "Have you told Thomas yet?"

Kate shuddered, folding her arms over her chest. "Not yet. I'm being a coward, I know, but how do you tell a four-year-old that his daddy isn't going to be with him anymore?" She lowered her gaze. "Not that Paul has been much of a daddy, but he is the only father Thomas knows."

"It'll be all right, Kate." He repeated the words that he'd said over and over to her last night.

Kate looked up, her gaze unusually clear and forceful, reminding him of Caris. "Yes, it will be all right. Everything always is." She smiled. "Thanks, Alex. I don't know what I would have done if you hadn't been there for me."

He shrugged her thanks away.

"Is there anything I can do for you?" she said.

He turned away, his response automatic. "No, I'm fine."

"No, you're not."

He turned to her, forcing himself to laugh unconcernedly. "Of course I'm fine, Kate. Why would you think I'm not?"

She cocked her head at him and he got the impression she was really seeing him—not just the take-charge always-in-control older brother—but the real him. A man, on the verge of gaining, or losing, everything.

"You can tell me the truth, Alex. I won't break."

Caris had said the same thing to him. He hadn't believed either of them. "Kate, I don't know what you—"

"John's in on this, isn't he?"

He strove not to look as cornered as he felt. "John?"

"Nothing would make John leave the theater." Kate perched on the edge of the sofa. "Not a bad string of luck, not poor finances, not even me."

Her mouth twisted grimly and Alex suddenly remembered why his sister had chosen to marry Paul instead of the better man, John. Both had promised love, but only Paul had been able to ensure financial security, something Kate desperately craved.

Kate stared at him. "But John would leave the theater to help a friend. He'd do it to help you."

For once, Alex had nothing to say.

Kate clasped her hands primly in her lap, waiting. "Are you sure I can't help you with something?"

It was tempting to tell Kate everything, to enlist her aid in the facade that was rapidly becoming impossible to maintain. But then he remembered last night. Kate, weeping in his arms, on the verge of returning to a husband she hated simply because she feared not being able to take care of herself or her son. If he told Kate the truth—the real truth—she'd go back to Paul.

No, he couldn't tell her the truth. But he could use her help in the negotiations. "Actually, Kate, you can help me." He leaned against the desk. "I'd like you to sit in on the negotiations."

Kate seemed to shrink before his eyes. "I'm not a lawyer, Alex. I wouldn't be any help to you at all."

He stood before her and took her hands in his, feeling them tremble. "Don't underestimate yourself, Kate. You would be a big help in there."

"No, Alex, really. I wouldn't be any help at all," she repeated. "Why don't you have Michael join you?"

Alex grimaced, knowing he couldn't tell Kate he didn't trust his own brother not to sabotage the deal, a deal meant to benefit all of them. "Kate, I need you."

She stared at him, aghast. "Alex, really. You don't need me. I wouldn't do anything but make a mess of things." Her eyes held desperate appeal. "Please don't make me do this."

He stared at her. When had his little sister become so doubtful of her own abilities? "Kate, you're an equal partner in Navarro Investments, and I think it's time you helped to run it."

"Me?" Her voice squeaked. She shook her head, curly black hair flying. "No, I couldn't..."

"Yes, you can." He placed his hands on her shoulders. "You're stronger than you think, Kate."

She frowned. "Where is all this coming from, Alex?"

"What do you mean?"

"A month ago, when Father died, you weren't pushing me to help with the company. Why now?"

He stared out the window, picturing Caris staring up at him through half-closed eyes, her golden hair tangled in his fingers. He remembered breathing in the scent of her until he didn't know if he could breathe without her.

Or live without her.

"Alex?"

He took a deep breath. "I want a life of my own. Michael has his women and parties, and you have Thomas and a renewed relationship with John." He watched a slow blush heat her face. "I want something of my own, too."

"Why don't you ask Michael for help? Isn't that why you asked him to come back?"

Alex's muscles stiffened. "I didn't ask him to come back. Who told you that?"

"Michael."

Alex closed his eyes. "Of course."

Kate laughed hollowly. "I can't believe I fell for another of his lies. You'd think by now I'd stop believing anything that comes out of his duplicitous mouth."

Alex was startled by the vehemence in her tone. "What?"

Kate sighed. "Michael is an arrogant, sarcastic, mean son of a bitch, and even though he's my brother, I don't like him very much."

"Kate!"

"It's true! He can be a real jerk. And he makes me feel stupid."

"He can make me feel stupid, too, Kate," Alex said gently. "I guess that's Michael's gift."

"He should exchange it for something else. It's not an endearing quality."

Alex pressed his palm to the back of his aching neck. "When did all this happen?"

"You mean Michael becoming a jerk?" She ran her hand along the mahogany bookshelf. "I think it happened the summer you left for college. It affected us all, but I think it affected Michael most of all." She turned back to Alex. "At least that's when I started to notice it."

Alex nodded, wondering if the family ties that had been broken could ever be mended.

"Alex?"

"Yes?"

"You'd tell me if there was anything wrong, right?"

Alex looked at Kate, seeing a flash of strength beneath her fragile exterior, a strength he'd always known was there. Still, he couldn't tell her the whole truth. Not yet, anyway. "Of course, Kate."

"You know you could tell me anything, and I'd keep your secret, don't you?"

He tried to appear flippant, unnerved at how close she was to the truth, but couldn't pull it off. He nodded stiffly. "I know, Kate. I know."

12

CARIS STARED across the broad mahogany table that served as the negotiating table and wondered when her life had turned into a soap opera.

She was sitting across from her lover, except she had to hide the fact. She had to pretend she didn't care for him, pretend she didn't want to touch him, pretend she only wanted a signature from him.

Caris sighed. She wanted so much more from Alex than his signature on a contract.

Her sexuality, dormant and repressed for the past eight years, silently screamed for recognition and acceptance. Caris felt as though her nerve endings were on fire. On the outside, she was calm and collected; inside, she twitched like a Mexican jumping bean.

She was even more tense than the day she quit smoking. She hadn't known it was possible to feel worse than that.

Her career was in jeopardy, her future was on hold, and she desired a man she couldn't have.

The door opened. Kate stood in the doorway. As everyone turned to look, Kate blushed. She waved her hand jerkily in an embarrassed greeting. "Hi. Sorry I'm late. Thomas ate a bug."

Harrison gasped. "Is he all right?"

Kate looked surprised by Harrison's question. "He's fine, thanks."

Alex patted the chair to his left. "Sit here, Kate."

"You can't be serious," Michael muttered.

Alex merely glared at him.

"I believe we are ready to start." Harrison nodded to Caris.

Caris reached into her briefcase and pulled out five copies of the land-deal proposal. She stood and handed them around the table. "Obviously, this is just a rough draft of the agreement."

"Obviously," Michael muttered.

She faltered at his sarcastic tone, but forced herself to go on. "If you'll open to the first page, you'll see we've outlined the financial aspects of the deal..." She looked up to see Alex staring at her, his brown eyes devouring her. His contract lay unopened in front of him; his attention was focused only on her.

Caris sank weakly into her chair, unable to go on in the face of Alex's hungry expression. "Harrison, perhaps you'd like to continue?" She hid behind her own copy of the proposal.

The senior partner cleared his throat and stood, adjusting his suit jacket. "Page one, paragraph one, line two..."

She flicked her gaze to Michael, then looked away quickly. Alex watched her. Caris shivered and turned her head away.

Harrison read aloud, oblivious to the tension around him. Alex turned the pages of the prospectus, but his eyes, hungrier than a hawk's, never left Caris's face.

Caris tried to look everywhere but at him. She burned with emotions that had nothing to do with her life as a lawyer. While Harrison droned on, Caris peeked around the table. No one was paying attention to the recitation of the terms. Caris well knew that a contract was never signed until it had been picked apart word for word in private, but usually, the opposing side was polite enough to pretend to be listening.

Alex caught her eye and winked. She pretended she didn't see.

Kate's confused gaze flitted between Caris and Alex.

Oh, boy, Caris groaned inwardly.

ALEX TRIED to force himself to concentrate on what Harrison was saying, a common courtesy he always extended. His gaze returned automatically to Caris.

She looked beautiful today. She had accented her pale blue suit with a single strand of pearls around her neck. It reminded him of the day he'd met her. A day that had changed his life.

He watched Caris's eyelids flicker as she strove not to glance at him. He forced his attention back to the legal proposition.

What he wouldn't give to throw everyone out of the room and make love to Caris on the big mahogany table. His hand caressed the smooth wood, wishing he was caressing her instead. He had never touched her in sunlight. He wondered if she would taste different.

"...if you'll just sign here, then."

Alex blinked quickly, realizing Harrison had finished his speech and was standing in front of him.

"I'd like a few minutes to review the document, Harrison."

Harrison frowned, but twisted the pen closed. "Certainly. Why don't Caris and I wait outside and you can discuss it with your partners."

When Caris stood, the silk of her stockings whispered softly to him. He felt her perfume softly touch him. He willed his gaze not to follow her, his body not to react. His body ignored him.

Caris left, closing the door behind her. Alex released a shaky breath.

"What is going on here?" Kate asked.

"You can't be serious about signing this," Michael said at the same time.

"What's going on between you and that lawyer?" Kate asked.

"We're giving them everything and getting almost nothing in return," Michael said.

Alex flipped through the contract, skipping the legalese that meant nothing and found the heart of the document quickly.

He waited until both Kate and Michael had stopped speaking before replying. "Michael, we've already discussed this, and Kate, it's none of your business what's going on between me and Caris."

Kate gasped.

"That's a fine way to treat your sister!" Michael said.

Alex looked at him, imagining his hands around his brother's neck. "You're a fine one to talk about our sister! You've done nothing but belittle and—"

"Please." Kate placed a hand on both of their arms. "Could we just deal with this contract and leave the rest of the discussion for later when we don't have two hungry lawyers waiting outside our door?"

They both stared at her.

"Don't look so surprised." She laughed. "I am a mother, capable of dealing with childish arguments like yours." Kate pointed to the contract in Alex's hands. "It sounds fine to me."

Michael snorted. "Forgive me if I don't accept your opinion as law, Kate."

"Enough." Alex spoke quietly.

He read through the rest of the document, then closed the contract with a soft sigh. "It's not good enough."

Michael slapped the table. "I knew it! So when do you want me to contact Nakashimi?"

"Nakashimi?" Kate asked.

Alex held up his hand. "It's not good enough yet."

"What more is there?" Kate asked.

"Look here." Alex flipped open the contract, and pointed to a paragraph on the second page. "Here they've agreed to build a medical clinic, but they've conveniently left out the training for local medical personnel, as well as an emergency medical-training program for personnel throughout the island.

"And here," he went on, "they've agreed to build a high school, but haven't added provisions about upkeep, materials and teachers' salaries. They're only offering half of what we asked for."

Kate tapped the contract with one finger. "So, what do we do now?"

Alex pulled out his pen. "Negotiate."

"Are you sure you want to negotiate with these people, Alex?" Kate asked. "They seem so...underhanded."

"There's nothing underhanded about this contract, Kate," Alex said. "Think of it as a game. Their objective is to get as much out of us while paying as little as they can. Our objective is to get as much as we can without giving up too much."

Kate looked doubtful. "I don't know if I'd trust them, Alex."

"Maybe Kate's right," Michael said.

"What?" Alex tried not to laugh, reading Michael's strategy clearly.

"Who says we can trust these two?" Michael asked. "I say we take our time, try to find another buyer."

"No, Michael. I'm not selling the beach to anyone who will destroy it. I'd rather not sell it at all than have it disappear all in the name of progress."

"But, Alex, think of the money," Michael said.

"What money? And who is Nakashimi?" Kate's gaze flew between her two brothers.

"Michael wants me to sell the beach property to Nakashimi Corporation, a group of Japanese investors who will tear down the town, making the people of our island homeless."

Kate wrinkled her nose. "Why would you want to do that, Alex? I thought you were creating a partnership to make sure the people have a future."

"Exactly," Alex said.

"Tell her the whole truth, Alex."

Kate waited.

"Nakashimi has offered more money—"

"*A lot* more money," Michael interjected.

Alex glared him into silence.

Kate pressed a hand to her forehead as though fighting off a headache. "This is all so confusing. I don't think I'm cut out for the business world."

"Sure you are, Kate," Alex said. "What are your instincts telling you?"

Kate paused and then said, "My instincts tell me to pick a buyer that will help the people as well as give us a healthy profit margin." She grinned. "I read about profit margins in Paul's *Money* magazine."

"That's exactly what business is about," Alex said. "Maximizing your profits without compromising your ideals."

Michael snorted disbelievingly. Alex turned to him. "Sounds like you have something to add, Michael. Why don't you just say it?"

Michael looked as though he was going to speak, but clamped his mouth shut.

Alex turned to Kate again. "Next thing to do is draw up a list of our concerns about the contract. We need to think about everything we want, then prioritize them. We probably won't get everything on our list, but we can make sure we get the things we really want. And, of course," Alex said, "there are always deal breakers."

"What's a deal breaker?" Kate asked.

"A deal breaker is something you can't compromise on. You either get the concession, or the deal is off."

"Do we have one of those?" Kate asked, nodding toward the contract.

"Yes," Alex said. "Here, on page nine, the contract states that ten percent of the resort workforce will come from the island. That's too small. I want to build the resort to provide job opportunities that allow people to stay on this island."

Kate nodded. "I see. So, where do we start?"

Alex pulled out a pad of paper and handed it to her. "Let's make our list."

CARIS CHEWED on her fingernail, watching Harrison pace the small hallway.

"What's taking them so long?" Harrison asked.

"He's probably reading the contract." Caris placed her hands in her pockets so she wouldn't continue to nibble on them.

"I read him the contract," Harrison said. "Why does he need to read it again? It was very specific."

Caris shrugged. They both knew no one signed a contract without reading it at least once more. Besides, Alex had had other things on his mind during the contract recitation. He hadn't been thinking about the deal. He had been thinking about her.

"Harrison?"

The senior partner stopped pacing. "Yes, Caris?"

"Harrison, I just wanted you to know that no matter what happens during the rest of our negotiations, I tried my best. Win or lose, I did the best that I could."

Harrison's gaze was intent and Caris felt that he was finally seeing her as a lawyer instead of just a female. He patted her arm. She was unnerved by the contact. It was so unlike the man, but she didn't pull away; she sensed he was trying to be nice.

"You're a good lawyer, Caris," Harrison said, surprising her further. "No matter what our differences, your work has been exemplary."

"What about the partnership?" Caris asked.

Harrison paused and she waited out the silence, forcing herself not to speak, knowing that in the world of business, the person who spoke first usually lost.

"It's up to the board," Harrison said finally. "But, as for myself, I have already made my decision."

Then he smiled at her.

She was so surprised she almost didn't see Michael open the door.

"We're ready for you."

CARIS REREAD Alex's list of demands.

"It's outrageous!" Harrison paced the floor of his suite.

"Actually, Harrison, there's nothing here we hadn't anticipated."

She handed the list to Harrison, who slowed his pacing long enough to grab it.

"It's no big surprise he wants a higher quota of employees from the island," Caris said. "There's nothing unexpected there."

Harrison sat down and stared at the list. He tugged at his tie. "You're right, of course. I just don't want to give away more than we have to."

"Me, too, Harrison."

"Let me look at this again."

Caris waited, her mind wandering back to her night with Alex.

After the deal is signed, I'm coming to claim you.

She shivered in anticipation. If Alex acted true to form, this affair was far from over.

"Why are you smiling?" Harrison asked.

"What?"

"You're smiling. Why?"

She forced herself to frown. "I just got excited about the deal."

Harrison nodded. "It hits me like that, too. Every time. The sweet smell of success. It's addictive."

Something was addictive, but she knew it wasn't the deal.

Harrison glanced at his notes. "Knowing what you know about Alex, what do you think he'll be obstinate about?"

Caris forced her attention back to business. "I think he'll expect some compromise in each of these areas. As far as a deal breaker, my guess is it would be the resident work quotas. Why don't we draw up some numbers and see what he throws at us?"

Harrison leaned forward and rested his elbows on his knees. "Now I know why I picked you to be my assistant." He smiled, a smile that reminded Caris of the smiles on her childhood dolls—false, painted-on.

She returned his smile, not wishing to spoil the mood by reminding him he hadn't picked her at all.

CARIS SLID the revised contract toward Alex's side of the negotiating table. "As you can see, we've been quite generous."

Alex glanced at the paper, then back at her with a smile that made her heart flip-flop. "Very generous, indeed. But not generous enough."

He scribbled a number in the margin of the contract and passed the paper back to her.

"No," Harrison said, reading over her shoulder. "There is no way we can guarantee we'll hire that large a percentage of workers from the island. What if they're not capable of doing the job?"

"Then we'll train them," Alex said.

Harrison pushed the paper back toward him. "We can't agree to that."

Alex pushed his chair back from the table. "Then we don't have a deal." He stood, staring at Caris.

"You're just going to walk away?" Harrison asked.

Alex nodded, his gaze leaving her and falling on Harrison. "The job quota is something I can't compromise on."

Kate stood next to him. Although she appeared awkward and out of place, her face shone with the excitement of the negotiations.

"I'll have to think about it," Harrison said.

Alex glanced at his watch. "Time is running short, Harrison. I'd like your answer after dinner."

Alex left the room. Kate followed so closely she looked like a puppy being walked on a too-short leash.

"He's not serious, you know," Michael said, still seated at the table.

"He sounded serious to me," Caris said.

Michael shrugged. "He's just trying to be a hard-ass. Throw in some extra numbers on the other parts of the deal and he'll agree to your terms. You'll see."

"Alex was very insistent," Caris said pointedly, knowing Michael was trying to sabotage the deal.

But why shouldn't she let him do it? All she had to do was sit back and wait. Harrison would listen to Michael, thinking he had the inside track on Alex's negotiating tactics. Harrison would refuse to budge, convinced that was the way to win. Alex, on the other hand, wouldn't tolerate Harrison's obstinacy. Alex would break the deal rather than give up the conditions he wanted.

Caris and Harrison would return to Washington without the deal. Michael would get his way. Caris, who could truthfully say she'd tried to convince Harrison to compromise, would become the firm's youngest female partner ever. And no one would ever have to know about her indiscretion.

Everyone would get what they wanted.

Everyone but Alex. And the islanders.

"Harrison, I..."

She told herself not to be stupid. She had nothing to gain by saving the deal.

Both Harrison and Michael turned to her. "Yes, Caris?" the lawyer said.

She shook her head. "Nothing."

Michael grinned and she felt herself burn. She was tempted to tell Harrison the truth about her and Alex just to watch Michael squirm. But that would be professional suicide. She bit her lips, biting back the words.

Michael stood and winked at her. "I'll see you tonight at the negotiating table."

He closed the door behind him.

"That was a surprise," Harrison said.

"Too much of a surprise, don't you agree, Harrison?" Caris asked. "I think he wants something from us."

Harrison gathered up the contract. "Of course he wants something from us. Everyone does. I'll bet he wants one of those high-paying positions on the resort's board."

She stared at him. "The man is rich. Why would he want to work for someone else?"

"Power."

Caris frowned. "How much more powerful can he be? He already controls half the island."

"Michael doesn't control half the island," Harrison corrected. "*Alex* does. Michael is simply a part owner of the company. I bet he probably has very little say in what Navarro Investments does. My guess is he wants to find someplace he can call his very own."

"I don't believe that, Harrison. I don't trust Michael."

Harrison walked toward the door. "You don't have to believe anything, Caris. I'm the one making the decisions, and I say we do as Michael suggested."

As the door closed behind Harrison, Caris knew the deal was dead. Harrison planned to remain firm. And Alex would never agree to his terms.

In a few days, she could return to Washington, to a new partnership with nothing but a healthy tan to remind people she'd even been on Navarro Island.

Michael was right. No one would blame her. The deal's failure would fall on Harrison's bony shoulders.

All she had to do was sit back and wait.

She had everything she wanted. She had nowhere to go but up.

So how come all she wanted to do was cry?

13

ALEX STARED across the table, the contract unopened in front of him. "I'm not bluffing, Harrison. When I said I wouldn't sign the contract without those quotas being raised, I meant it."

Harrison sighed theatrically. "Then I guess we don't have a deal."

Alex stood, knowing they had all lost. "I guess we don't."

A flicker of something that could have been panic flared in Harrison's dull gray eyes. "Really, Alex, *everything* is negotiable."

Alex stared at Caris, wondering why she hadn't impressed the seriousness of the situation on her boss. "Not everything, Harrison. Some things are too important to mess with."

Or to give up. I'm coming for you, Caris, he thought. Just as soon as this deal was completed, he planned a well-deserved vacation to Washington, one of his favorite cities. Except this time, he had no intention of coming back alone.

He turned to Kate who sat next to him, wide-eyed and openmouthed. "We're leaving, Kate."

"That's it?" she squeaked. "You're just going to leave it all because of one number?"

"There are some things a person can't compromise on." He held out his hand. Kate's glance darted between Harrison and Caris. "Can't you give in?" Kate asked Harrison. "Just this once?"

Harrison shook his head. "Like Alex said, some things a person can't compromise on."

Alex realized with a start that Harrison thought he was

playacting. That this deal really wasn't over, just entering a new dimension.

He glanced at Caris. The blank, slightly dazed expression on her face told Alex that Caris knew this deal was dead. So why wasn't she doing something to save it?

He gave it one more try. "Harrison, this isn't some negotiating tactic. I'm serious."

"So am I."

Alex shook his head. Nothing he said now would help. He left the room, not bothering to check whether Kate was following him or not.

He stripped in his bedroom and threw on his swimsuit, hoping to ease his tension in the ocean. He had gambled and lost, and the people of Navarro Island were going to pay the price.

When he returned from his swim, his muscles burning with exhaustion, his brain still whirring over the situation, he was surprised to find Kate waiting in his bedroom.

"I can't believe you did that," Kate said.

Alex rubbed his hair vigorously with a towel. "And hello to you, too."

"I'm serious, Alex. Look at me!"

She stood in front of him. Her hands were bunched on her slim hips, her feet turned out as though she were digging her heels into a patch of dirt. She was ready for a fight.

Alex fought not to laugh. The last time Kate had looked this determined had been fifteen years ago. Michael had just beheaded her Barbie doll collection and Kate wanted justice.

"I told you, Kate. There are some things that can't be compromised. You knew the job quota issue was important to me. Why are you so surprised?"

She stared at him. "But, Alex, the money..."

"What about the money?"

She lifted her hands in appeal. "You can fool Michael, Alex, but you can't fool me. I found out about Dad's debts."

He didn't have to ask her how she knew. And he really

couldn't blame John for telling her. A man in love did stupid things. Look at what he himself had done.

Kate lowered her voice. "Once the will leaves probate, everyone else will know about them, too."

Alex threw his towel on the floor. "Would you rather have me sell out the islanders so we can remain wealthy?"

"No, of course not. But might not the people at Nakashimi be willing to compromise a bit?"

Alex gaped at her, bitterness coating the inside of his mouth. "Has Michael talked to you about this?"

"That's not fair! I only did what I thought was best for all of us."

The pit of Alex's stomach tightened and burned. "What have you done, Kate?"

Kate flushed and looked away.

He placed his hands on her shoulders. "Whatever it is, you can tell me."

When she stared at him, her eyes were wild. "Tell me the truth, Alex. Are you in love with her?"

"Yes."

Kate closed her eyes. "Michael said you would do anything for her, but I never thought..."

He wanted to shake her. "What did Michael tell you, Kate?"

She pulled away and walked toward the patio window, staring out at the ocean. "Michael said you were making a deal with Caris because you were sleeping with her, even though Nakashimi's deal was a better offer. I didn't believe him, but then when you wouldn't take Harrison's offer and Caris did nothing to convince you, I started to wonder if we were going to get anything at all." Her voice faded to a whisper.

"Tell me what you did, Kate."

She grasped his arm pleadingly. "I have to take care of my son, Alex."

"Tell me, Kate."

She dropped his arm. "Michael said we were broke."

"We're not broke, Kate. Even after the will is out of probate we'll still be able to take care of ourselves. Barely, but we'll be okay."

"But—"

"I'd never let anything happen to you or Thomas, Kate. Trust me."

She was silent, seeming to consider his words.

"Tell me what you did, Kate," Alex repeated.

Kate cocked her head and assessed him. "Are you happy, Alex?"

"Happy?"

"With her?"

Alex smiled, thinking of Caris.

"Yes, I think you are." She turned away. "I'm sorry, Alex, but I gave my vote to Michael. He's gone to Houston to make a deal with Nakashimi. I'd give anything to take it back."

Alex closed his eyes with a groan. Damn his brother!

"He told me Thomas and I would be broke, and then I'd have to go back to Paul. He sounded so convincing," Kate said in a tiny voice.

"He always does," Alex murmured. He strode to his closet.

"What are you doing?"

"I'm going to fix this." Alex pulled out the most powerful business suit he'd brought.

"How can I help?" Kate asked.

"I need you to stall Harrison. No matter what happens, don't let either of them leave." He turned to her, his stomach burning. "Especially Caris. I need you to make sure she doesn't leave."

"Why would Caris leave?" Kate asked. "I thought she was in love with you."

He closed his eyes in pain.

"She's not in love with you?" Kate whispered. "Oh, God, Alex. How can she not love you?"

Alex stared at his closet, seeing a barren future without Caris. "Turn around, Kate, so I can get dressed."

She did as he asked. While he dressed, he said, "I think Caris is in love with me. She just hasn't realized it yet. We're perfect together." He pulled on his pants. "She makes me happy, and I know I bring her peace." He pulled on one shoe, hopping for balance. "But she's stubborn."

Kate took a deep breath. "Do you think Caris will like us?"

Fully dressed, Alex placed his hands on her shoulders and turned her to face him. "How could she not love you, Kate?" He kissed her cheek. "I do."

She hugged him tightly. "Are you really happy, Alex? Have you thought of how this will change your life?"

He imagined a life where he never had to be alone again and grinned. "I can barely think of anything else." He kissed her forehead. "I'll be back soon."

CARIS STARED at Harrison, feeling as though the next few minutes were going to decide the rest of her life.

"He's lying," Caris said.

Harrison frowned. "Who are you talking about?"

"Michael. He's lying."

"Why would he lie to us?"

"Why would he help us?" Caris asked. "You said it yourself. We can't trust any of them."

Harrison sat in his room, his fingers fiddling with his drab, brown tie. That meant he was thinking.

"You've done the research, Caris. Tell me what you think I should do."

Caris took a deep breath. It was rare for Harrison to ask anyone's opinion, especially a junior attorney's. She had to choose her words carefully.

"I think you should believe Alex when he says he won't compromise. Research has shown he never bluffs. When he says he plans to do something, he always follows through."

Harrison paled. "I've made a mistake, haven't I?"

He looked vulnerable and Caris realized how important this deal was for Harrison. Martin Joffrey often joked that Harrison Peters was due to be put out to pasture.

Caris realized now that it was no joke.

If Harrison didn't come through with this contract, Martin Joffrey would force him out. Retirement wasn't a dirty word, except to someone like Harrison Peters, who had no life outside of his office.

People like that didn't retire to Florida.

People like that didn't retire.

They died.

Caris shivered. One more incentive for her to follow her heart.

"Don't worry, Harrison. I'm sure we can fix everything. If we rewrite the proposal and add enough terms Alex wants, I'm sure he'll sign it."

"We've got some work to do then, don't we." He smiled crookedly, and reached for the copy of the contract.

Hopefully, Caris thought, *this won't be the last thing I do for Harrison, Harrison, Joffrey and Peters.*

She concentrated on the contract to keep from worrying about what would happen once Michael discovered she had resurrected the land deal.

"MICHAEL DOESN'T HAVE a majority vote for Navarro Investments," Alex said six hours later, leaning on the business table in Nakashimi's Houston office. "I do."

"Don't listen to him." Michael jumped up from his seat, panic tingeing his voice. "He's just mad because Kate and I aren't going along with his plans."

Alex pulled a paper out of his suit jacket. "I have here a sworn deposition from Kate Navarro giving me her share of voting privileges." He glared at his brother. "What do you have, Michael?"

"Her word," Michael said, staring down his brother.

"Words don't hold up in court, do they?" Alex said. He

turned to the investors who were silently listening to their exchange. "Michael, if you try to push this deal through," Alex said, "I'll drag you into court. And," he added, pausing for effect, "I'll win."

The oldest Japanese man stood, followed immediately by the others. "I'm sorry for the mix-up, Mr. Navarro," he said. "We were unaware that we were doing business with the wrong Navarro family member." He held out his hand. "We would appreciate it if you didn't advertise our misunderstanding."

Alex shook his hand. "I understand."

With a polite nod to Alex, the Nakashimi executives left the room.

"You did it again, didn't you?" The softness of Michael's voice was at odds with the anger flaring in his eyes.

"Did what, Michael? Stopped you from committing fraud? Didn't you realize that once Kate discovered you lied to her, she'd remove her vote? What would you have done then?"

"I could have convinced her again." Michael sounded much the way he had at fifteen when he'd tried to bluff the school bully into not beating him up.

"Give it up, Michael. You made a mistake. A big mistake, and you got caught." Alex motioned with his hand. "Come on. Let's go."

"Go where?" Michael asked in an angry and clipped tone. "Back to *your* house, *your* school, *your* world?" He jerked his head. "I don't think so."

Alex dropped his hand. "Is that why you left school? Because I went there first?"

Michael flushed. "Why I left school is none of your business, Alex. Just like the rest of my life is none of your business."

Alex strove to keep his voice calm. "What do you want, Michael?"

"I want my own life, without you in it."

"So do it. Nothing's stopping you."

Michael snorted in disbelief. *"You're* stopping me, Alex! You're always ahead of me. First on the island, then at Harvard, now with Nakashimi. Why don't you just leave me the hell alone?"

"Because you're my brother and I love you. No matter what you do or how badly you try to hurt me. You're my family until the day I die."

Michael twitched. For a moment, Alex wondered if his brother was going to cry. "We're nothing to each other, Alex." Michael shouted finally. "Do you hear me? Nothing!"

Alex's voice was soft. "No, Michael. We're not nothing. We're brothers. And that's stronger than any land deal." He sat in one of the chairs. "Sit down, Michael. Let's talk."

"No. We're nothing, Alex. Not even brothers."

"Michael..."

He was gone before Alex even made it to the door.

14

THE NEXT DAY, Caris attached the printer cable to her laptop computer and hit a key to print the revised contract. The machine began to whir just as someone knocked on her door.

"Good timing, Harrison. The contract is almost printed."

But it wasn't Harrison on the other side of the door. It was Michael.

"What contract?" Michael asked with a suspicious gleam in his eyes.

This is it.

Caris swallowed nervously. "Harrison has decided to give in to Alex's demands." She tossed her head in a defiant gesture.

"And just who convinced Harrison, I wonder?" Michael asked softly. He clenched his fingers into an angry fist and Caris forced herself not to flinch.

"Hello, Caris. Michael."

Harrison stood in the doorway. Caris's heart beat a staccato rhythm. She took a deep breath, trying to control the nervous tremors vibrating throughout her body. She smiled although her lips were stiff with panic, and pulled the contract from the printer tray. "Here is the revised contract you asked for, Harrison."

"I wouldn't take that if I were you," Michael said.

Damn. Caris's heart sank and her hands began to shake. The contract in her hands whispered a nervous symphony.

"What do you mean, Michael?" Harrison asked.

"Your partner is a traitor."

Caris gasped. "I am not!"

"What?"

"Think about it," Michael said. "She convinced you to give Alex more concessions, didn't she?"

"We thought it would be the only way to get the deal accomplished." Harrison sounded annoyed that he had to defend his actions. Or hers.

"They suckered you," Michael said. "My brother is bluffing. He and Caris are working together to get more money out of your firm." Michael cocked his head, looking like a devious puppy dog. "Haven't you wondered why Caris hasn't been as hard-nosed as usual?"

"Because that style of negotiation won't work with your brother," Caris said. "Alex Navarro doesn't give in to strong-arm tactics."

Michael arched one eyebrow. "How do you know?"

She wanted to slap him. "I know because I've done my research, Michael."

"Who are you going to believe, Harrison? An owner of Navarro Investments—" he glanced pointedly at Caris "—or Alex Navarro's lover?"

Caris groaned. *This was it.*

"What?" Harrison's glance shuttled between the two of them. "What is he talking about, Caris?"

"It's not what you think, Harrison..."

Michael chuckled dryly. "Oh, yes. It is what you think, Harrison. Ask her."

All eyes turned to Caris.

"Is this true, Caris?" Harrison sounded as though he wanted to believe her.

"Yes, but—"

"I told you." Michael grinned.

Caris burned with embarrassment and despair.

Any remaining hope Caris had disintegrated when Harrison turned to face her, his expression telling her he'd expected this action, and worse, from a female attorney. "I'll expect your resignation by this afternoon."

"That's it? Just like that, I'm out?" Caris asked incredulously.

Harrison turned toward the door. "It's too bad, Caris." His voice was wistful. "You would have made a good partner."

Harrison closed the door with a final click.

"Why did you have to do that?" Caris turned on Michael, wishing she had long, brightly colored fingernails she could use to scratch his eyes out. "Just because you screwed up my life doesn't mean your deal is going to go through. Alex will never agree with your plans. And after I tell him what you did..."

Michael leaned toward her, his brown eyes lit by rage. "You don't have to tell him, Caris. Alex already knows."

"What?" She stepped back, confused. "I don't believe you."

"Think about it, Caris." Michael's voice sounded almost kind. "Did you think it was just luck that I knew you and Alex had made love?" He clucked his tongue against his teeth in a condescending and irritating manner. "You can't be that naive, can you?"

"Alex wouldn't do that to me."

Michael cocked one dark eyebrow. "Wouldn't he? Why not? Alex got exactly what he wanted."

"What are you talking about, Michael?"

"We knew you'd be the tough one," Michael said. "That's why Joffrey sent you, isn't it? To be the voice of reason. Harrison's too temperamental. You, you're pure ice."

Ice Queen.

She felt like throwing up.

Michael reached out to touch her cheek.

She flinched.

"With you out of the picture, Harrison knows he'll have to take the full blame if this deal doesn't go through. He's willing to do almost anything to ensure it does go through. Fear is a powerful motivator. Especially for a man like Harrison."

Caris shivered. "I'm going to talk to Alex."

"He's not here."

"What?"

Michael smiled, reminding her of a snake about to devour a mouse. "He really doesn't have the stomach for this sort of thing. Face the facts, Caris. You lost. Why don't you just scurry back to D.C. and clean out your desk. I'm sure you'll have no trouble getting another job. Why, if you asked nicely, Alex would write you a nice reference."

You can work anywhere, Caris. Alex's words from the night they made love taunted her.

"I don't believe you." She pushed her way toward the door.

"Fine. See for yourself," Michael called after her. "I'm just trying to stop you from being hurt."

Caris raced into the hallway.

"Where are you going?"

Caris jumped. Kate stood next to her.

"I'm looking for Alex."

"He's not here."

"What?" Her stomach constricted. "Where is he?"

Kate glanced around guiltily. "I don't think Alex wants me to tell you."

Caris sank weakly against the wall. So it was true. The brothers had played her against each other, all for the sake of the deal. She wanted to drop to the floor in tears but didn't want to give any Navarro the satisfaction of seeing how much they had hurt her. Caris folded her arms and adopted the tough stance she'd practiced in preparation for her first court case. "Do me a favor and tell Alex it was fun."

Kate's mouth dropped open. "You're leaving?"

Caris shrugged. "You win some, you lose some. Tell him it was great doing business with him."

"But how can you leave?"

"Easy. Harrison asked me to resign. I'll swim home if I have to."

"But I thought you and Alex were—"

"Alex and I are nothing. And you can tell him that for me."

Kate stepped forward. "I really don't think you should leave."

"Try to stop me."

Caris heard a car in the driveway and panicked. What if it was Alex, returning to finish what Michael had started? Just how much heartache was she supposed to endure? She raced into her room and threw everything in her suitcase while Kate watched from the doorway.

"What are you doing?"

"Take a wild guess." Caris flung the suitcase under her arm and hurried toward the door.

"Wait!" Kate grabbed her arm.

Caris tried to fling off Kate's hand but couldn't. For a tiny woman, Kate was remarkably strong.

Caris dropped her suitcase and whirled to face Kate. She gritted her teeth. "I'm warning you, Kate. Either help me get out of here, or get out of my way."

"Do you love Alex?" Kate asked, still holding Caris's arm.

Yes! Caris's mind shouted, but she forced herself to laugh, a tough, cynical laugh. "Love Alex? Are you crazy? Why would I love the man who ruined my whole life?"

Caris heard the car door slam and knew she didn't have much time to get away. "Tell Alex to stay out of my way or he'll be sorry."

Kate gasped. "You'd actually hurt him?"

No! But Caris nodded vehemently, afraid to trust her voice to another lie.

Kate grabbed the handle of Caris's suitcase. "Come on. I'll drive you to the airport myself."

CARIS SAT in the Houston airport, an unopened cigarette package on her lap, and listened as an impersonal voice recited a list of departure gates. She tried to concentrate on the speech. Anything was better than reliving what had happened over the last few days.

It was impossible. Her mind kept returning to Alex.

Alex.

Where was he? What was he doing? Did he know she had left?

Did he care?

Her fingers played with the cellophane wrap on the cigarette package. This is what she had been waiting for. A chance to smoke a cigarette in peace. The bet with Alex meant nothing anymore. She had no intention of ever seeing him again.

Caris turned to look as the door to the smoking lounge opened. The air looked hazy and foggy. And dirty.

She tucked the cigarettes in her pocket. She didn't want to smoke. Maybe she was too upset to have a cigarette.

Or maybe she didn't need them anymore.

When she first began smoking, Caris hadn't even enjoyed it. But she had endured, sensing it was a way into the old boys' club. Perhaps it was not only time to give up the old boys' habit, but to give up on the old boys themselves.

She shook her head and joined the long line of passengers boarding the jumbo jet. She had to face the truth. Her career at Harrison, Harrison, Joffrey and Peters was dead. She had never really fit in there, anyway. If she had, Harrison wouldn't have asked her to resign. He would have at least given her the chance to explain.

In Harrison's world, Caris would always be a female lawyer, when all she really wanted to be was a lawyer.

Caris could find another job in another law firm. She had professional contacts, people who would vouch for her character and brilliance. Harrison wasn't likely to spread around the true reason she'd resigned. Instead, he would cite personality differences or some other innocuous excuse.

Caris knew the role she'd have to play in order to land another position: that of the brilliant, pseudomale attorney willing to relegate her personal life to her career.

But did she want to do that anymore?

Caris stared out the window at the waiting plane. After letting Alex into her life, Caris felt different. Revitalized. Alive. It was as though the real Caris Johnson had been hiding inside attorney Caris Johnson. And now that her true self had been liberated, she didn't want to imprison her again.

She had been dead for so long. She should thank Alex for opening her eyes to the life she was missing.

Perhaps. One day. When it didn't hurt so much to even hear his name, silent as a prayer, in the back of her mind.

Caris gazed out again, noticing the interplay of white clouds and blue sky.

Thoughts of contract law and land deals didn't interest her anymore. She wanted to make a difference. She wanted to make a difference in *other* people's lives. She wanted to practice a different kind of law. She wanted a job in which she could effect change.

She wanted a job that mattered.

The answer came out of nowhere. Matthew Clark.

Odds were, her socially minded law-school buddy hadn't found a new law clerk. And he'd often told her she'd make the perfect partner.

Partner. The word sounded different to her. In the past, partner meant power suits, meetings behind closed doors and money. Now, she heard tones of cooperation and support she'd never sensed before.

Partner. They would help each other. She would help Matthew by providing affordable legal assistance to the people who usually couldn't obtain it, and maybe Matthew could give her a reason to be happy in a world without Alex.

Alex.

Her stomach tightened in yearning for him. Had it only been a game to him, as the law had been a game to Caris? Or did he feel some emotion for her? Had she reacted too quickly?

Or had the night that changed her life meant only lust and power to him?

Caris didn't know what to think anymore. Her brain thudded with the noise of her thoughts.

She closed her eyes and concentrated on slowing down her breathing. She envisioned cool air filling her lungs as cigarette smoke had once filled them.

Matthew had taught her that, nearly a decade ago. He'd been convinced that meditation would teach Caris patience. She'd tried it once, then told him it took too long.

She hadn't meant it as a joke and had been offended when he laughed. At the time, she hadn't understood why he'd laughed. Now she did.

Caris took a deep breath, held it for a few seconds, then exhaled slowly.

Was Matthew's office still the same ramshackle closet a few streets from their old campus? Had the winters in Connecticut improved any? Or would Matthew finally be able to teach her to enjoy the peace and quiet of a snowbound afternoon?

Was Matthew's hair still a ponytail of premature gray and silver? Caris hoped to emulate Matthew's serenity, but she doubted she'd ever understand his preference for ponytails or year-round sandals.

Caris found herself heading for the pay phone. But her hand wobbled while the phone was still in its cradle.

She couldn't decide the fate of her life on a whim. She had to think about it, weigh all her options as well as the pros and cons of this plan. She had to make charts and graphs. This would take days, not mere minutes.

Caris had always been logical where decisions were concerned. *And look where that's gotten me*, she thought. Brokenhearted and jobless.

She picked up the phone.

This time, any deals I make are going to come from my heart.

The first person Caris called was her secretary at Harrison, Harrison, Joffrey and Peters.

"Hi Caris!" Linda said. "Have you signed the deal yet?"

Caris swallowed grimly. The bad news hadn't reached her office yet. "I'm no longer employed by HHJ and P," she said, trying to sound optimistic.

"What?" Linda lowered her voice. "Was it the red bikini that pushed Harrison over the edge?"

Caris laughed. "Something like that. I took your advice, Linda. I acted like a woman instead of a lawyer."

Linda drew in a sharp breath. "I'm so sorry, Caris. But, you don't sound upset."

"Actually, I'm not. I feel remarkably free. I've decided it's time I act like myself."

"It's about time!" Linda said. "I'm happy for you. But I'll miss you. Even though you were one of the more productive members of this firm and worked me to death, I always liked you, Caris."

"Thanks, Linda. Could you do me one more favor?"

"Sure."

"I've decided to move. I'm not coming back to Washington. Could you clean out my desk and pack everything in a box for me? I'll send someone by to pick it up."

"Sure." Linda lowered her voice until it was barely a hiss. "What do you want me to do with your client files?"

Caris knew what Linda was asking. "Nothing. The firm retains control over all my clients and the work I've done while in their employ."

"Officially, that's true," Linda said, "but this is the real world, Caris. I repeat. What do you want me to do with your client files? I could copy them and no one would know except me and the copy machine."

"No thanks, Linda."

"At least let me send you a list of clients. You know that most of them only deal with Harrison, Harrison, Joffrey and

Peters because of you. You could have your own practice ready to go."

Caris took a deep breath, wobbling on the cusp between her old life and her new. "I don't want a practice like that, Linda. Thanks, but no thanks."

They announced boarding for her flight. "I have to go now, Linda. I'll call you in a few days."

"Good luck, Caris."

Caris replaced the phone, surprisingly elated by the new turn her life had taken. She pulled her hair out of its bun. From now on, she was a new Caris Johnson. And this time, she was going to have some fun.

"I WON'T SIGN THIS."

Confusion coated Harrison's pale face as he stared at Alex. "Why not? I've given you everything you asked for. What more is there?"

"Caris Johnson."

"What?"

Alex let his hand glide over the cool, smooth negotiating table, remembering how warm and smooth Caris's skin had felt. "I understand you asked her to resign."

"Ms. Johnson acted...improperly."

Alex turned to him, his anger barely controlled. "What do you mean, improperly?"

Harrison blushed. "You know. *Improperly.*"

"I don't understand, Harrison."

Harrison sighed. "I don't blame you for taking advantage of what Caris so wantonly offered, but I do blame her. Caris is a lawyer and she had no business sleeping with you."

"*What?*"

Harrison's eyes blinked rapidly behind his bifocals. "Didn't you and she...?" His voice trailed off.

Alex closed his eyes, understanding suddenly.

Michael.

Alex crossed his arms, rage at his brother's manipulation

making his arms shake. "Michael lied, Harrison." Alex tightened his jaw, wishing it was a noose around his brother's neck.

"If Michael was lying, why didn't Caris deny it?"

"Would you have believed her?"

"Probably."

"Probably not," Alex said. "I think you believe that just because Caris is a woman, she can't be a good attorney."

"I never said that," Harrison blustered.

"But you might as well have," Alex said. "And that's where you made your mistake."

Alex turned toward the door. "Unless you get Caris Johnson back and give her the partnership she deserves, we don't have a deal."

"What if she won't come back?" Harrison asked, his voice warbling.

Fear gripped Alex's heart like a fist. What if Caris didn't come back? She had to. He couldn't imagine his life without her.

"You'd better make sure she does, Harrison. If not, you'll be on your way back to Washington, without having made this deal."

Alex slammed the door, startling John in the hall. "Where's Michael?" he bellowed.

For once, John was speechless as he pointed toward Michael's bedroom.

Alex threw open the door to Michael's room and stood in the doorway, his blood boiling.

Michael jumped up. "It's not my fault she left!"

Alex stormed into the room and grabbed Michael's collar in a fierce grip. He squeezed the material, wishing it was Michael's throat instead. "I've had it with your interference and petty plotting, Michael. One of us is leaving, and it's not me."

Michael paled. "You're kicking me out?"

He sounded so much like the hurt boy he'd been at eight that Alex released his grip and stepped back. "Isn't that what you want, Michael? Your own life without me around to mess it up?''

"You'd really throw me out of the family?"

Alex reached out and Michael flinched. Alex dropped his hand, the chasm between them widening. "How did this happen, Michael? We used to be close."

Michael's shoulders drooped with a sudden weariness. "I want it to stop, too, Alex. All I ever wanted was to be a part of Navarro Investments. All I wanted was a little responsibility."

"Why didn't you just tell me what you wanted?"

"I did." Michael flushed, his anger returning. "At least I meant to. But you were always so on top of every deal, that I thought I never stood a chance. I also thought that whatever deal I did touch would crumble like dust." He dropped his eyes. "Look at how badly this turned out."

"Not so badly."

Michael's eyes were wide with astonishment. "What are you talking about? Of course it turned out badly. Caris lost her job, I lost Nakashimi and you lost your deal. What else could go wrong?"

Alex shook his head. "Harrison and I have tentatively agreed on a deal and Harrison told me he'd give Caris the partnership she deserves. I'm glad we lost Nakashimi. We didn't want them anyway."

"I wanted them."

"Did you really? Or was it just a way to get back at me?"

Michael cocked his head, considering. "Maybe you're right."

Hope expanded in Alex's chest. "Once I'm married, I don't plan on spending all my time on the business."

"You're going to marry her?" Michael asked. "I thought you were just having an affair."

Alex suddenly remembered why he wanted to murder his brother. "If we're going to get along, Michael, you're going to apologize to Caris for what you put her through. What exactly did you tell her?"

When Michael opened his mouth to speak, Alex held out a hand. "Stop. I don't want to know. The way I feel now, I'll probably do something we'd both regret."

Michael closed his mouth.

"I'll ask you later when I've calmed down. Maybe when I'm eighty and a great-grandfather."

Michael smiled weakly.

Alex rubbed his forehead, frustration folding around him like a vise. "Michael, promise me that, no matter what happens, you won't go over my head and try to subvert any of our business deals."

Michael nodded.

"We're brothers, Michael, and I love you. But I swear, if you *ever* do anything like this again, I'll kick you out of the company, the family and the whole state of Texas. Agreed?"

"Yes. I'm sorry this happened," Michael said, looking more ashamed than Alex had ever seen. "It started out as simple rivalry. I was just trying to outdo my older brother. But somewhere along the way, I started to think I really hated you, and then, it was hard to remind myself that I do care about you." Michael straightened his shoulders and faced Alex, his gaze clear and strong. "I won't let you down, Alex. You can count on me."

"I'm sorry I never listened to any of your ideas, Michael."

Michael shrugged. "Why should you? I never gave you any reason to." He shook his head ruefully. "But that's about to change. I'm going back to school. Maybe they'll still let me take my finals. And when I graduate, we can be real partners."

Alex patted his brother's arm, relieved to see that this time Michael didn't flinch. "Good." He looked at his watch. "I have to go. Harrison and I are leaving for Washington."

"How can I help?" Michael asked.

"Hope Caris is willing to be my wife," Alex answered grimly.

"And if she isn't?" Michael asked.

"Then you and Kate better learn how to work together. Because the two of you will be ruling owners of Navarro Investments and I'll be trying to convince Caris. Wherever she is."

15

I'VE COME FULL CIRCLE, Caris thought, looking around the studio apartment she'd moved into only a few days earlier. It was more than its proximity to Yale University that reminded her of her college days. Like her old abode, it was spartan, and contained a kitchen barely big enough for one cook. And like her college pad, it could only accommodate a single bed.

Not that I need a bigger bed, Caris thought with a wounded sigh. *No one's going to be sleeping in it but me.*

The familiar loneliness washed over her, drowning her in regrets. She knelt in front of the boxes the movers had delivered this morning, unwilling to be defeated by emotions she couldn't heal.

Caris ripped open the box labeled Kitchen Utensils. She was curious as to what was in there. As far as she could recall, the only items in her D.C. kitchen had been an empty refrigerator and an unused stove.

The box contained a new set of pots. A gift from Linda. Caris opened the card:

Hope you're going to learn how to cook in your new life.

Love,
Linda.

P.S. The salt and pepper shakers are in the bottom of the box.

Caris picked through the box, laughing as she found them. The saltshaker was a ceramic female torso spilling out of a red bikini. The pepper container was a muscular male torso, barely contained in black bikini briefs.

Caris swallowed and shook her head, remembering another male in black briefs. She caressed the smooth surface, feeling the pull of loss she wondered if she'd ever overcome.

She missed Alex. It had been nearly two weeks since she'd left Navarro Island. She'd read in the *Wall Street Journal* that Harrison and Alex had sealed their deal just a day before news of Alex's father's debts surfaced.

Lucky Alex; he had gotten exactly what he wanted. And in a way, so had she. Harrison had come crawling back and had seemed surprised, and more than a little offended, when she turned down the chance to wind up negotiations on the Navarro deal and become a partner at the firm. He'd told her the door was always open to her, but she hadn't even left him her new phone number. That part of her life was over. And she hadn't smoked in two weeks. *That* was good.

Sorrow stung her. Despite everything that had happened, she missed Alex. She should accept that she would never hear from him again. But each time the phone rang, her heart raced. Each time she heard a man's voice, Caris dared to dream it might be Alex coming to get her.

Coming to claim her.

After this is over, I'm coming for you.

But he hadn't. She sighed. He never would.

Her eyes stinging with now-familiar tears, Caris placed the ceramic salt and pepper shakers on the avocado-green countertop and stood back to survey them. She was absurdly pleased by them.

Caris turned to the unpacked boxes, hoping to lose herself in something besides thoughts of Alex.

She wept when she unpacked her lingerie collection. There would never be anyone she could share that part of herself with. She had given her heart to Alex.

Caris ached to be touched. But she only wanted Alex to touch her. She ached to be loved. But she could only imagine Alex loving her.

The tears started anew. Caris sniffled and forced herself to concentrate on her new life and not the life that ended the day she left Navarro Island.

On the plus side, Caris loved her new job. She and Matthew were a great team. They complemented each other beautifully, even though she still wore business suits, and Matthew's ponytail was twice as speckled with gray and twice as long as it had been in college.

Someone buzzed her apartment and Caris stood and wiped her dusty hands on her new jeans. She glanced at her watch. Matthew was early. He had promised to bring some of their clients to help paint her apartment. Afterward they were all going to a Latin dance club downtown. Matthew was convinced he and his Latina wife, Graciela, could teach Caris to salsa.

Caris didn't believe him, but she was looking forward to the evening out, her first since returning from Navarro Island. She even planned to wear her red dress, the one she had previously worn only in the solitude of her D.C. apartment.

She threw open the door. "You're early, Matthew, but come on in."

Caris's mouth flew open.

Alex stood on the other side of the door, his face a cold mask. A muscle ticked in his cheek, the only thing that assured her he was alive and not some hallucinatory image.

"Alex!"

"Who's Matthew?" He stepped into the apartment.

"Matthew?" She shook her head, trying to clear the sudden fog.

"Who is he?" Alex asked.

"Matthew?"

"Yes, Matthew."

"He's my new partner. What are you doing here?"

"Partner," Alex repeated gravely. He tilted his face toward the ceiling so she couldn't read his expression. "Harrison told me you turned down his offer of partnership." His gaze landed on her, as searing as a live electrical wire. "And you wouldn't even give him your phone number. Why?"

"I didn't want to."

Alex frowned. "It's a partnership, Caris. Harrison told me he even got you a larger profit-sharing margin. Didn't he tell you?"

Caris crossed her arms tightly, needing to hold on to something. "He told me. I still turned him down. Alex, why are you here?"

Alex remained silent, his gaze devouring her.

Caris turned away, unable to bear his scrutiny any longer. "Would you like something? Tea? Coffee?"

She stepped into the tiny kitchen, aware that Alex never moved.

She searched the cupboards, seeing nothing, concentrating only on the silence behind her. Had Alex left?

Had he even been there?

She heard him shrugging out of his overcoat and let out a relieved breath.

His hand dipped in front of her and reached into the cupboard. She jumped back. She had never even heard him move.

Alex pulled a jar of instant coffee from the cupboard. "I'll make it," he said. "You look like you're going to pass out any minute. Sit down."

"I don't want to sit down!" She did sit, though. Her legs were wobbling and couldn't seem to hold her up.

Alex puttered around the kitchen. It was a sight that should have seemed strange to her, but didn't.

"What are you doing here?"

He frowned. "Why do you keep saying that? You know why I'm here." He found the plastic spoon she'd gotten at some fast-food place and placed coffee granules into the oversize mugs Matthew and Graciela had given her as a housewarming present. "We signed the deal."

"I'm happy for you," she said, unable to keep the bitterness out of her voice.

He closed the coffee jar and turned toward her. "I told you I'd be back once the deal was signed. Don't you remember?"

"I didn't really believe it."

"Why not?" He abandoned the coffee and hunkered down beside her, his hands balanced on her thighs. His fingers ignited a fire she thought would never blaze again.

Caris closed her eyes, afraid to look too closely into his eyes. Afraid of what she would see. "Do we really have to go over this, Alex? It's over and you won. Isn't that enough for you?"

"I didn't win, Caris. I lost everything."

Her eyes flew open. "But, the deal? Harrison said you got everything you wanted. Enough to pay off all your father's bills without touching any of the money in Navarro Investments."

Alex smoothed her thighs with his hands, an action Caris didn't think he was even aware of.

But she was. Wherever he touched, she burned. She squirmed in her seat, wanting him far away. Wanting him closer.

"I got the deal." Alex's brown-eyed gaze held hers with a force as potent and unwavering as gravity. "But I lost you."

Suddenly Caris couldn't breathe. Or she didn't need to. Who needed air when she had this?

"I love you, Caris, and I want to spend the rest of my life with you." He kissed her softly. She tasted her tears on his lips.

Alex traced the path of her tears with a gentle fingertip. "Do you still hate me?"

"I never hated you, Alex."

"But you told Kate—"

"I was angry. And hurt. I thought you had used me. I just said that so she'd let me leave before I made a fool of myself and begged you to let me stay."

He kissed her again, licking away the salt of her tears. "I wish you hadn't left. Then I could have done what I planned to do."

"What's that?"

His gaze was solemn. "The moment I met you, Caris, my life changed. I became greedy—greedy for a life and a love of my own." He picked up her hand and kissed it, an oddly formal gesture, yet a surprisingly sensual one. "Caris, will you marry me?"

Caris's chest swelled with emotion. She was so overwhelmed, she was unable to speak. She framed his warm face with her hands and kissed him, trying to convey her love the only way she could.

Alex grinned. "I'll take that as a yes."

He lifted her effortlessly in his arms and kissed her until her bones melted and Caris could barely remember her own name.

A LONG TIME LATER, they lay on her single bed, Alex's overcoat serving as a blanket. They hadn't been able to locate the sheets quickly enough and had covered the bed with their own discarded clothing instead.

Caris placed her head on Alex's chest and heard the reassuring thump of his heartbeat beneath her ear. His fingers were tangled in her long hair, soothing her with long, rhythmic strokes.

"I like your hair like this," he murmured.

"You mean loose?"

He chuckled. "No, I mean splayed over my naked body."

She smiled. "So, where do we go from here?"

"Wherever you want."

"What do you mean wherever I want? Where do you want to go?"

He kissed the top of her head. "The most important thing is that I have you as my wife. Everything else is incidental."

She propped herself on his chest with one hand so she could look him in the eyes. "What about Navarro Island? And your family?"

Alex leaned forward and kissed her. "You're my family now, Caris. They'll have to learn to take care of themselves.

They'll be fine." He brushed his rough cheek against her smooth one, making her shiver at the gruff massage. "It's my turn to live now."

"But you've worked so hard to make this beach resort a reality. How can you give it all up?"

"I'm not giving it up," Alex said. "I'm just stepping aside. It's time someone else put their lifeblood into the island. For now, I plan to use my energies elsewhere."

Alex stroked her back in a rhythm that was as arousing as it was soothing. He lowered his voice until it sounded as though he was reciting a prayer. "I've waited my whole life to find you, Caris. I'm not going to risk losing you by not being with you. You are the number one priority in my life. And you always will be."

"But what about the islanders?"

"They'll be taken care of," Alex said. "Kate's promised to help out developing the resort until Michael gets his degree and can take over. Then, depending upon how things go with John, she's thought about trying her hand as a set designer. Painting is her first love." He winked at her. "As was John."

"John? And Kate? Wow. Who knew?"

Alex kissed her. "There's lots you don't know, Caris. But I'll tell you all about it later."

He pulled her to him, and there was no more talk as their bodies communicated for them. By the time Alex pulled away, Caris was breathing heavily and had forgotten what they had been talking about. Then she remembered.

"I have a deal for you," she said.

Alex's eyes twinkled. "That sounds intriguing. Do we get to negotiate?" His hand sought out her naked breasts.

"No negotiations. Just better priorities. You once told me I could get a job anywhere. Is there a job for me with Navarro Investments?"

Alex's eyes widened. "This won't be a fast track to a corporate partnership, Caris. Even if you are the president's wife."

Caris placed a finger over Alex's lips, urging him to be silent. She replaced her finger with her lips and kissed him gently. "That's not important to me anymore, Alex. I'd rather have a job that makes a difference in the world. And I'd rather be with you."

"Working on the island resort is going to take a lot of hard work and a lot of time—and it will provide few financial rewards."

Caris smiled and curved her hand over Alex's heart. "I have all the rewards I need right here. I'll need a few weeks to find Matthew a new partner, and then I'm all yours."

He chuckled.

"What?"

"I just can't figure you out, Caris."

"Is that so bad?"

He grinned. "It will make life interesting. But tell me something. When we first met, all you considered was the bottom line. Why the change?"

She laid her head back on his shoulder and threaded her fingers through the deliciously coarse hair on his chest. "All my life I've made decisions using only my intellect. And look where it got me. Alone, lonely and afraid of my own body."

She sighed. "No, Alex. This time, I'm dealing from the heart."

He circled Caris with his arms, providing a haven she knew she would always treasure. "As long as it's a heart that loves me, I'm happy."

"I love you, Alex."

"And I love you, Caris."

The doorbell rang.

"Damn!" she said.

Alex propped himself on his elbows. "Who's that?"

Caris laughed. "Our timing is terrible!"

"What do you mean?"

Caris jumped up, ran to the door, still naked, and peeked through the spy hole.

She scurried back to bed. "Right now," she whispered, one

hand on his chest, "there are eight guys standing outside my door with paintbrushes and wallpaper paste."

Alex reached for his pants. "I think I'd better get dressed."

Her heart sank. "You're leaving?"

He kissed her. "Never. But I'll feel more comfortable meeting eight guys if I'm dressed." He tossed her shirt to her.

The doorbell rang again. "Coming!" Caris yelled, pulling the shirt over her head. "I know you just got here and all—" she jumped into her panties "—but I promised Matthew we'd go dancing tonight."

Alex grabbed her and dipped her as if he was Fred Astaire. He kissed her, making her head spin. "I may be liberal, Caris. But I'm not that liberal."

Caris giggled, her head still spinning from their impromptu dance. "With Matthew and his *wife*." She touched his throat softly, the only part of him not covered by clothing. "I want to go, Alex. You see, there's this red dress I have in my closet that I've never gotten to wear and—"

The doorbell rang again and he kissed her quickly. "I don't think we have time to talk about your clothing, now, Caris. But whatever you want to do is fine with me."

"Whatever?" She thought of the lingerie she'd thought no one would ever see.

"Get dressed, Caris," Alex growled, sounding like a sexy tiger. "Before I take off my clothes again."

She giggled and wiggled into her jeans.

"Ready, Caris?"

Alex held out his hand and she placed her hand in his. He squeezed her fingers.

"Ready for anything," Caris said.

It's hot...
and it's out of control!

It's a two-alarm Blaze—
from one of Temptation's newest authors!

This spring, Temptation turns up the heat. Look for these bold, provocative, *ultra*-sexy books!

#679 *PRIVATE PLEASURES*
Janelle Denison
April 1998

Mariah Stevens wanted a husband. Grey Nichols wanted a lover. But Mariah was determined. For better or worse, there would be no more private pleasures for Grey without a public ceremony.

#682 *PRIVATE FANTASIES*
Janelle Denison
May 1998

For Jade Stevens, Kyle was the man of her dreams. He seemed to know her every desire—in bed and out. Little did she know that he'd come across her book of private fantasies—or that he intended to make every one come true!

BLAZE! Red-hot reads from Temptation!

Take 4 bestselling love stories FREE

Plus get a FREE surprise gift!

It's a dating wasteland out there! So what's a girl to do when there's not a marriage-minded man in sight? Go hunting, of course.

Manhunting

Enjoy the hilarious antics of five intrepid heroines, determined to lead Mr. Right to the altar— whether he wants to go or not!

#669 *Manhunting in Memphis*— Heather MacAllister (February 1998)

#673 *Manhunting in Manhattan*— Carolyn Andrews (March 1998)

#677 *Manhunting in Montana*— Vicki Lewis Thompson (April 1998)

#681 *Manhunting in Miami*— Alyssa Dean (May 1998)

#685 *Manhunting in Mississippi*— Stephanie Bond (June 1998)

She's got a plan—to find herself a man!

Available wherever Harlequin books are sold.

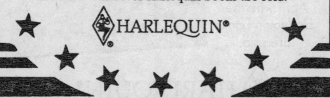

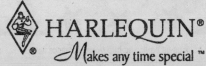